DAY OF THE RAVEN

Eyes Of Midgard Book 1

Lee Dawna

LeeDawna Books, Inc.

First edition

Cover design by Premade Ebook Cover Shop

https://www.premadeebookcovershop.com

ISBN 978-1-949192-31-5 (paperback)

ISBN 978-1-949192-30-8 (ebook)

Published by LeeDawna Books, Inc.

https://leedawnabooks.com

leedawnabooks@gmail.com

P.O. Box 205, MacArthur WV 25873

~

This book is dedicated to my patient, long-suffering podcast listeners.
This is only the beginning.

~

There's not a single remarkable thing about Sean Winkle, and yet he resisted my magic in the woods, fought off Keela's compulsion, broke through the wards on our home, and somehow wielded enough magic to step into the pocket world my ancestors created thousands of years ago. Never in the recorded history of my people has a human ever crossed into our world.

Sean – *Six hours earlier*

Last night was darker than most. I spent the vast majority of it out on the deck of the home I've lived in my whole life, looking up at a sky so thick with clouds that not even the light of a late August moon could break through. Still, I sat underneath stars I knew were up there and talked to my parents. I told them about how I used the funds from the sale of our house to pay for tuition at Merrymont University, the college they'd be proud of me for getting into because going to Merrymont was always the dream. Mine and theirs. A dream that for the last seven years felt more like an impossibility because the one thing none of us factored into our dream was death. It came for our family, though. First taking my dad, and after a six year battle with cancer, taking my mother from me only eight short months ago.

I park Dad's old pickup truck in the student lot on the east side of campus where it sticks out among the array of sports cars and highly polished trucks with their lift kits and fancy wheels. Merrymont isn't Ivy League, but getting accepted here is harder than getting into Harvard. I know because I applied there, too. Their tuition isn't as steep as Merrymont and Harvard also offers scholarships, but I didn't want to attend a college simply because my hard work during high school would afford me a free ride. What I wanted was Merrymont. Ever since second grade when Collin MacKenzie wore a blue t-shirt with the college's logo on it to school. I asked what the three interlocking triangles stood for and the rich little prick told me it stood for a college where dummies and ankle biters with names like *Sean Winkle* weren't allowed. I punched him in the mouth hard enough that he swallowed a loose tooth. We've been best friends ever since.

I step out of the truck and tug my oversized blue and gray duffle bag from the bed. This is the one thing that I let myself splurge on when I got Merrymont's acceptance letter. This bag now holds the contents of my entire life, complete with sheets and a blanket my grandmother quilted for her *sweet young man* when I was thirteen. I sling the strap over my shoulder. After Mom passed away, I began the process of packing up our house. Furniture and clothing went first. I sold some and donated others, and even left a few things for the new owners who were gracious enough to let me stay in the house until this morning. It was hard walking away from the only home I've ever known, but when Mom was alive, she used to tell me that she knew in her heart I would make it to Merrymont. That I belonged here. After she died, the only thing I knew was that without either of my parents, our house didn't feel like home anymore.

I walk across the parking lot and step onto the lawn of Merrymont University, taking my first big inhale of the future. For as dark as it was last night, today is bright, cloudless, and so warm it feels like the beginning of summer rather than the cusp of fall. I tilt my face into the sun and give my parents a smile. If there's a way, I know they're watching me right now, and smiling just as big as I am. We might not have been rich like the MacKenzie family, or any of the other wealthy elite in our small town of Richlands, but between Dad's job at the car lot and Mom working in the water company's office, we lived comfortably enough. Better than that, we had no shortage of joy. Right up until Dad was killed in a freak accident at work and it took all of his life insurance and every penny of our savings to battle the cancer Mom was diagnosed with the following year. "I made it," I whisper to them. "I'm going to make you proud."

With my face still in the sun, I take a step. A body bounces off my broad chest. I grab for the lanky frame, collecting a handful of the old man's suit jacket while the rest of him collapses into a puddle of skin and bones in the grass at my feet. I drop the fistful of material so his arm isn't cockeyed and kneel down beside him. *Great way to make a first impression, Sean.* There are few reasons for a man his age to be on a college campus and despite this being freshman move-in day, I doubt this is merely someone's grandfather. "Are you hurt?" I ask the likely professor as I grip his jacket-clad elbow and help him into a sitting position.

He wipes his wrinkly hands over his scratchy black trousers. "If knocking me down will get you to pay attention to your surroundings, then I guess not."

I bristle. I already feel bad for knocking him down and it wasn't entirely my fault. He wasn't paying attention to his surroundings either. Plus, I'm a little over six feet tall and this man is at least that, so I'm surprised neither of us saw the other. "Sorry," I offer him my hand and help him regain his feet, trying to get a good look at who is underneath the wide-brimmed hat that's keeping his face shrouded. All I can tell is that his face is long and punctuated by a broad chin. Judging by the fact that he's dressed like it's winter instead of an unseasonably warm day, I assume he's fairly old. "Are you a professor here?"

His head dips, blocking even the shadow of his face from my view. "Of a sort."

I swallow. He's an adjunct professor then, and I really hope he isn't the instructor in one of my classes. "What do you teach? Maybe I'll get another chance to apologize to you in class."

He chuckles, the sound strong and virile, not as weak as he appears. "East of the sun, west of the moon, my boy. When you seek The Third, you must go east of the sun, west of the moon."

I readjust my bag, hoping this man didn't hit his head when he fell. "Um, okay. Is there someplace I can help you get to?"

He laughs again, ambling away. I go after him but claws dig into my head. I swat at the bird, missing it completely as the raven dives toward the ground in front of me, banking off to the right and flying away. I watch as it climbs higher with each beat of its shiny wings, heading toward the student center.

I run my fingers through my thick mop of sand-colored hair. I've got that natural bedhead look that the ladies seem to like. It's short enough not to be out of control and yet long enough to encourage women to run their fingers through it. Once I figured out they like that sort of thing—and muscles—I dedicated myself to the latter and let the former work its magic. Not to be a player but because I was the poor kid in my neighborhood. With the absence of money, I gave myself other redeeming qualities. A necessity in circles where people as handsome and wealthy as Collin were the norm. I don't usually get birds mistaking me for their nest, though. In my twenty-two years of life, this is the first time a bird has ever tried to land on my head.

I muss my hair again, making sure the bird didn't leave any gifts behind while turning back to check on the old man. He's gone. I crane my neck to look between the rows of cars. I don't see him and as tall as he is, I should be able to. I guess he's inside one of the vehicles now and with any luck, he isn't the driver. With a second shot of that luck, maybe he won't be one of my professors. Merrymont is a small school but not so small that I can't avoid bumping into the whacky professor again. All I need to do is heed his advice and pay attention to everything around me. I've worked too hard to get here to blow it. Especially on my first day.

I stroll toward the student center, keeping one eye on where I'm going while also taking the time to scan the nearby buildings with their blue flags hanging proudly from the eaves. Each one is embossed with a gray letter M that's set overtop an interlocking trilogy of triangles. All over campus, the patios and greenspace are laid out in that same interlocking triangle shape. The aerial photographs I've seen online are stunning. "Sean!" My name rings out above the din of freshman arrival day. Straight ahead of me, Collin is strolling down the spacious left branch of the patio in front of the student center, arms open wide as if he's Christ himself come to greet me. If Collin took his shaggy brown hair out of the ponytail tied at the nape of his neck, he and his ruddy, sunbaked complexion would probably even look the part. "My man, you finally made it!"

I set my course to intercept his, throwing a quick glance around at the benches spread here and there, some tucked into the landscaped center of the triangle. Part of the beauty of this campus is the way nature and stone weave together, the decorative landscaping as much a usable part of campus as the buildings. There are trees with thick branches that have been trained and trimmed into shapes that allow them to be used as chairs or tables and students are doing just that. Every part of campus is being utilized in some way, including the thigh-high stone walls rising up to encase the patio.

I watch the reactions of the quartet of girls perched in the grassy area just beyond the wall Collin is currently walking past. One of them has long red hair in a braid that falls to her waist. Of all the people glaring at Collin, her eye assault is the worst. I get it. He's loud and intrusive, and more than one person has had to duck to keep from getting whacked by his outstretched hands. All without so much as an acknowledgment from the offending Collin. People have a right to be grumbling insults, and the redhead has a right to glare at him any way she likes, but oddly, what I appreciate most about Collin is that he's always been true to his prickish nature. That's because he isn't being a jerk on purpose. Most of the time, he has no idea he's being a donkey's rear. Collin's behavior is a product of how he was raised. Once I met the rest of his family, I immediately understood that. Collin is the *nice* MacKenzie, based on a rating system that's only applicable within his family. Outside of it, he's exactly what he is right now, a selfish prick who doesn't really care if he accidentally slaps a girl in the face. In his mind, it would be her fault because she didn't move out of his way. I reach him and bring him in for a hug, one hand clapping against his while the other stretches around him. "I know you're happy to see me but you don't have to whack anyone upside the head to show it."

He chuckles, his bright white teeth sparkling in the sunlight. "I might have gotten a little too close to a few cheeks but I can't help myself, this is college. You finally made it!" He clamps his palms over my shoulders and shakes me. "I've waited three years for you to get here. Now I get to show you around and I already have a party lined up for tonight."

My chuckle matches his and I'm sure my smile is just as big. I've been so overwhelmed with emotion today that I'm not sure if what I'm feeling is better expressed by getting on my knees in gratitude or climbing onto the rooftop and shouting. "Trust me, I'm as excited about me finally being here as you are. Before I party with you, though, I need to get checked into my dorm."

He gives me a shove. "Dude, no. I let you stand on that crap about morals and not taking money from me to pay your tuition, so this is now our last shot at living the college experience together. You're not staying in the dorms. You're staying with me at the fraternity house. Since I'm the one sponsoring you, you're basically already in anyway."

My jaw works. I do want to join Sigma Beta Λύκος but the other pledges will be younger and unfortunately for me, this is Collin's senior year. Growing up, the plan was for us to join together, me knowing I could only get in because of Collin's family pull. Sigma Beta Λύκος consists mainly of legacies and from what I understand, most of them are related to the MacKenzies in some way. Outside of those legacies, the only other pledges allowed in are boys coming from families with wealth or titles, preferably both. I don't come from that kind of stock and once Collin is gone, I'm sure at least some of the others will be hellbent on reminding me. "I already paid for a private room in the dorms. Besides, you told me your house is full this year."

He raises a brow at me. "Yeah, there's not an extra room, which is why you're bunking with me. I already put a cot in there for you and I already told everyone that when I'm gone next year, you keep my room. It's the best one in the house. We have a private bathroom and even a little sitting area, which is where I put your cot."

A bird squawks off to my left and I begin scanning the trees for the sneaky raven. "Classes start in two days. Let me get settled into the dorm and then I'll go check out what kind of makeshift bed you're trying to talk me into sleeping on." I drop my eyes and glare at him the way the redhead was earlier. "Unless you want to sleep on the cot and let me have the bed?"

He staggers away from me dramatically. "I sleep in a king for a reason. Sometimes more than one of them, so that dorm you paid for might come in handy after all."

I can't help but laugh. "That's what I thought. You love me like a brother until I cramp your style."

He snorts. "Nothing cramps my style, and I lined up some ladies for you, too. They're all coming to the party I'm hosting for you tonight and I told them to wear something sexy for my man. But not too sexy, because I know you like 'em sweet." He leans toward me. "If you decide to get it on with any of them, I'll let you have my bed for the night."

I open my eyes wide. "One night? How generous." He laughs but that blasted bird is squawking again and this time I spot the raven sitting on the top of the student center. It dives off the side, swoops low between the buildings, and disappears behind a row of meticulously trimmed pine trees. The random girls Collin is talking about are sure to be hot because he wouldn't have spoken to them otherwise, but the prospect of meeting any of them isn't why my heart is currently trying to escape my chest. My body is suddenly overheating because of the dark-haired girl sitting on the end of the wall. The sculpted white spruce are providing a striking backdrop for hair as black as the raven's wings. It's wavy and thick, the ends softly tickling over her shoulders as she looks down at the phone in her hand. I can't even see her whole face and yet every fiber of my being is yelling that it's her. *The one.* My forever.

I try to look away but my eyes won't let me. Try to remind myself that there's no such thing as love at first sight while fighting the urge to propose to this girl whose name I don't even know. Desire is building inside of me with each beat of my heart, and I don't need a college degree to know the reaction my body is having to this girl is unnatural. I have no choice but to go to her, and without Collin at my side because the jealous demon inside of me who I didn't know existed until this moment is chanting a murderous song. It will kill him if he touches her.

O ver the last four years, every step I've taken has been in contradiction to all of the childhood plans Collin and I made. I could have started at Merrymont the year after high school the same way he did but while his family spends money as if it grows on every tree in their hundred-acre estate, I've never taken money from them. My parents worked too hard, sacrificing all they could in order to make sure I was in the best school district and had nice clothes to wear. Taking a handout from Collin to pay my tuition would have felt like I was slapping them in the face. Now that I've spotted my future wife, I'm even more certain that I made the right choice. My late arrival at Merrymont might have ruined our childhood plans but had I come sooner, I might have missed her somehow. As bizarre as my physical reaction is, for the first time in a long time, I feel whole again.

"I'll see you in half an hour," I tell Collin, forcing my eyes to his so he doesn't see what I've just had the pleasure of beholding. I've never had a problem with competition but my dark-haired maiden is already drawing more than only my attention, and the fire in my veins grows worse whenever I think about one of the other males here getting to her before I do. If Collin is that male, there's an above-average possibility that he'll end up managing to insult her while simultaneously hitting on her. I've seen it happen too many times, and the absurd part of me that's already in love with her will then be forced to unleash the violence pulsing at the tips of all my nerve endings. "Get out of here, Col. I'm going to dump my duffle in my dorm and then I'll come over to your place."

He studies me, knowing me well enough to notice something is up. "You just got here. I'll come with you."

I give him a little shove. "I snagged a private room but I still have to use the communal restroom, so it's probably going to suck enough that if you fix up my cot, I might be persuaded to live there with you. On the nights when neither of us has company."

He points at me. "I like it. And since tonight is all about you, I'm going to go pack a bag because it looks like I'm living the dorm experience tonight!"

I watch him trot away while doing a final check of my hair, dragging a hand through it to reassure myself there are no nasty little gifts tucked into the locks. I don't need bird droppings in my hair when I approach this girl. I'm already going to have a hard enough time keeping the intensity of what I'm feeling from showing. I've been told that my green eyes are potent, and not always in the best of ways. I guess sometimes I look a little too aware, like I'm a predator intent on fixing my prey with an eerily intense stare. Thankfully I've only had a few females get creeped out by me. The rest of the time they seem to like that when I look at them, it's with the passionate awareness of a hunter. Even when that passionate awareness is unintended.

I walk toward my current prey, scanning the features of the girl perched on the wall a hundred feet in front of me. She's stunning. It's as if the world fed a computer the exact details of what they thought was beautiful and out came this girl, an impeccable rendition of timeless beauty with pale skin, wide eyes, high cheekbones, and the most perfectly formed crimson lips. I can already see myself kissing those lips while running my fingers down the nape of her long, elegant neck. *Keep it together, Sean,* I scold myself as I close in on her. My dark gray t-shirt is already sticking to my back and with how hot it is out here, coupled with how hot she is, it won't be long before my pits look like I took a hose to them. As gross as she'll probably find that, I'm staying my course. I don't want to hear her voice, I *need* to hear it. Everything inside of me is screaming that she's going to sound as good as she looks, and that I'm going to need to know her ring size.

As if agreeing with my internal assessment, my left hand begins to burn, heating from the knuckle of my ring finger and outward, as if I've just pressed the back of my hand onto a hot stove. I ball it into a fist and look for a bee sting but the skin is flawless. I shake out the offending hand and pick up my pace. There's no time to worry about reckless birds and bee stings. All I want is to scoop this beautiful woman into my arms and hold her in the place she belongs. Right against my heart.

If she's noticed any of the males whose radar she's pinged, she isn't giving them any attention. She looks bored and wholly uninterested in everything around her. That's good. If she so much as gave one of them a polite smile they'd probably misconstrue it as flirting and that would be all the encouragement they'd need. Instead of sitting around staring at her, they'd suddenly find themselves confident enough to approach her. I've never shared in their particular kind of lack of ego because while it can be humiliating when a woman shoots you down, never speaking up gets you exactly nowhere. I'd rather be assertive and forced to lick a wound than sit idly by never knowing if a girl might be interested in me. Especially this girl. *My future wife.* The one who'll probably tell me to get lost if I don't keep my newfound temper in check.

I rub at my jaw, glad I've never had to shave much because I didn't bother with it this morning, back when I was a normal human instead of this lust-crazed lunatic. Five feet away from her, I open my watering mouth. Any closer and I might as well get down on one knee because I'm already dying to taste those lips, and one of my rules has always been that I don't kiss on a first date. Collin says that makes me a prude but that's only because I never told him about kissing Bonnie Potter when I was ten. She lived a street away from me that year and I used to cut through the woods to her house. One day, she asked me to kiss her. I liked her, so I did. Right after, she asked me what I thought about her kissing skills, announcing that she'd been practicing on the frogs that lived in the little pond in front of her house. After that day, I went four whole years without kissing anyone else and I checked my mouth for warts nearly every day of that four years.

"Hi, I'm—"

The love of my life jumps from her spot on the wall and strolls away from me, her long jean-clad legs making short work of putting distance between us. I have to admit, she looks good from this angle too. Even her thin, delicate arms are sexy as they swing at her sides. The black tank top she's wearing crosses her back with slinky straps that allow me to admire a whole lot of her creamy skin. While I don't mind the angle, I do mind the distance. I don't want to admire her from afar. I want to get up close and personal with every glorious inch of her.

I take off after her, groaning as she disappears around the corner of the student center before I have a chance to catch up. I was hoping she was going inside. If I knew she wasn't, I would have jogged and caught up with her before she veered off the patio because now I look like some kind of weirdo stalker following her down an alley. At least it isn't dark. This day is bright and my future is clear. It's twenty yards ahead of me and moving with the sleek prowess of a panther. Now all I have to do is figure out when to run up to her, and what to say when I get there. *Marry me* feels right but despite my current situation, I'm not actually a moron.

I've studied the map of this campus for years. That was part of my wishful thinking even during the times when it felt like I'd never make it here, so I know every inch of this campus and even what lies beyond. The sidewalk we're on curves down between the student center and the library, dead-ending into a staff parking lot that's surrounded by a decorative nine-foot wall separating the lot from rows of off-campus apartments. Between the wall and the apartments is a small patch of trees. My dark-haired beauty looks to be my age so I'm guessing she isn't staff. She must live in the apartments. Which means I shouldn't keep following her. I should run back to my truck, drive over there, and camp out near the path that leads through the patch of trees until I see her again. If she's a student here, she'll eventually head back to campus and it will be slightly less creepy of me to happen to step out of my truck as she's walking by than for me to keep following those very tight jeans of hers into a dark and wooded area.

I hesitate, hanging back as she leaves the sidewalk and begins to cross the staff parking lot. My hand begins to itch, that burning sensation from earlier following the itch as it climbs up my arm. I take a step and both the itching and the burning begin to subside. I glance down at my hand to be sure I didn't somehow get into a nest of fire ants but there's nothing on my hand. No marks. No stings. Nothing. I shake it out and look back to where my girl is now closing in on the edge of the wall at the far side of the lot. I don't have the bandwidth to process whether or not the burning in my hand is a medical issue. I might be having a heart attack but the only thing my brain is concerned with is the distance between me and the love of my life.

I cross the parking lot, following her exact path down the length of wall to where a footpath cuts behind it and through the trees. I duck around the corner of the wall the same as she did and slow myself down to a snail's pace while allowing my eyes to adjust to the dim light. I can see the path but it's darker back here than I expected. Not the best environment to approach a woman in. I should probably hang back and wait to speak to her until we're through the woods and back out into the sun on the other side. For all she knows, I live in the apartments too. While I won't lie about living over there if she asks, I won't offer up the information either. After we get to know each other and she sees that I'm not a creep, I'll confess to stalking her today.

I heft my weighty duffle onto my opposite shoulder and wind along the trail that's barely wide enough for two people to walk side by side. A thick layer of thorny underbrush flanks the path, and above me the canopy is so full it's nearly impenetrable. I imagine this is the kind of place that makes a solo female uncomfortable. All the more reason to force my feet to keep this slow, steady pace. If I let my heart lead, I'll take off running to catch up with her and if she's not already scared, me running up to her will do the trick. I'm not exactly a small guy. In addition to my hulking frame, I also failed to even bother calling out to her before she disappeared behind the wall. I just skulked along behind her, shamefully checking out every thread of those curve-hugging jeans. I feel a physical connection to her, though, a deeply rooted love I never thought possible. Which is probably the kind of thing all lunatic stalkers convince themselves they're feeling. *You're going to Hell for this, Sean.* I scold myself for the second time today, and yet still pick up my feet and continue on my quest. I'll confess to Collin later and have him knock one of my teeth out. He's a jerk, but there are lines even he won't cross, and stalking is most definitely one of them.

I allow myself to shift up a gear in speed, walking at what I hope is still a nonthreatening pace as I watch the trail ahead of me. Despite her dark hair and shirt, I should at the very least be able to see her silhouette. If she's picked up on the fact that a creeper is behind her, she could be running right now. I should be able to hear that, though. It's unlikely that she'd choose to hide in the thorn bushes but if she did fling herself into the underbrush and I happen to see her, I'll have to keep walking and move past her because trying to convince her that I'm not a psychopath by scooping her up and carrying her out of the woods while professing my undying love is probably going to land me in jail.

I wipe at the sweat beading on my brow. It's very likely that I've botched this relationship before it ever got past introductions. A thought that causes rejection to pulse through my already burning veins. I have no right to feel this way. I have no right to *any* of the things I'm feeling, but logically knowing that is doing nothing to quell the inferno building in my chest. I want to stop my pursuit but I physically can't. I need her. For reasons that go beyond mere attraction. I'm not some horrible monster who thinks her beauty gives him a right to treat her like an object. She's a person with her own set of feelings and I'll respect her every wish. Right after I have a chance to plead my case to her because so help me, I can't live without her.

Leaves rustle on the path up ahead of me and I pick up the pace. A bird squawks from somewhere nearby but I don't look to see if it's the raven again because my dark-haired beauty is straight ahead and she's not alone. There's another silhouette in front of hers. She reaches for it and my feet plant themselves into the soft dirt of the path. A guy with shoulder-length hair so blonde it's nearly white dips his head down to hers, his shiny strands of hair mixing in stark contrast against her dark ones as they kiss. Her hands curl against his alabaster skin. She moves her body against his and his hands smooth down her sides to rest low on her hips. Flames whip wildly inside my chest, growing hotter as she pushes him backward, their mouths still attached as she shoves him against a tree and feeds her hands up under his shirt. That should be mine. Her touch. Her kiss. *Mine. Kill him.*

I suck in a gasp of air, the noise in my head growing loud and painful until every crevice inside of my skull is a raging inferno of jealousy. Possessiveness bleeds into my limbs, telling them to claim her. To kill *him*. The guy who is pressed against her lips, one of his hands cradling the back of her head as he holds her in place against his mouth and deepens their kiss. For as beautiful as she is, he's just as striking. His skin is as pale as hers, and everything about him seems to glow. From his handsomely chiseled features right down to his purple-painted fingernails. They make a good match and the thing clawing from my depths has only one command. *Kill him.*

My mouth goes dry, my whole body feeling like it's going to burst into flame. I need to get out of here, yet all I can do is watch them, unable to look away even though I know I'm only seconds away from following the raging beast's commands. As if he knows what's happening to me, the guy's pale eyes snap to mine. They aren't afraid, though. They're amused. He slides the hand on her hip down lower, running it slowly over her bottom and hoisting it up to fill his palm with a cup of her backside. My fists clench and my teeth grind. He might be enjoying himself now, but we'll see how he feels when I'm holding his decapitated head in my hand.

3

I unglue myself from the path, so consumed with my need to end the life of the boy touching what's mine that I nearly miss the sound of footsteps pounding over the ground behind me. I focus on the sound, using the presence of other humans to calm the murderous rage inside of me. The wrath still aches to break loose but the footsteps are enough of a distraction to force my foolish attention away from the lovers. I turn and look behind me. Three figures come into view, dashing all hope of me escaping these woods without getting blood on my hands. Their arrival might keep me out of prison but it's going to put me in the hospital. Which is what I get for being a creep. A beatdown by some of the largest men I've ever seen. The one in front is at least six inches taller than me, and like the other two, he's not wrapped in muscle the way I am, he's made of it.

I toss my duffle to the ground beside me. The flash of amusement in the eyes of the guy behind me now makes better sense. He wasn't simply enjoying the fact that he had a jealous audience, he was proud of himself for procuring the perfect bait. His girlfriend is crack to idiots like me and now that I've played into their game and allowed myself to be lured into this trap by a beautiful girl, he and his friends are going to rob me. From the angry looks on the faces of the three men marching toward me, they're going to make it hurt, too.

I flex my fingers. When I signed the final paperwork on the sale of my family's home, I left the lawyer's office and went directly to the bank. This semester's tuition was wired straight to Merrymont and the rest went into a savings account where I'll get a meager interest payment while that money sits around also waiting to be sent to Merrymont, the all-inclusive school where absolutely everything is included in the price of tuition. Even snacks, drinks, and all the meals you want in any of the three twenty-four-hour campus restaurants. Meaning I had no need to bring much cash with me. Not that I even have much left over after squirreling away the tuition. Me not being the typical rich kid at a college like this is sure to disappoint these thieves. The same as me fighting back will. But if they want the hundred dollars worth of tens in my wallet, they'll have to take it from me.

I step just off the path so that my back is flanked by the underbrush. I doubt lover boy is going to put his manicured hands into this fight, but just in case he's planning to hit me from behind, I'm not going to make it easy for him. I face the more immediate threats and brace for impact as the three newcomers continue their menacing march toward me. They look to be my age but they aren't frat boys and they're certainly not here to mess around. They're moving with purpose and covering ground with the kind of precision you don't get from doing keg stands or mugging college students. These aren't petty thieves. The air around them is practically vibrating with power. The kind of power that drives fear to settle into your bones.

I track the movements of the one in front since he's going to reach me first. His blonde hair is longer than that of the white-haired guy, flowing past his shoulders as if he should be shirtless and on the cover of a romance novel. In a beauty contest, he'd tie for second with the guy behind him. They're nearly identical, except the second one has his long blonde hair tied up in a ponytail, the sides of his head shaved. He's also closer to my height and sporting a face that's slightly less angry than that of his larger ticked-off twin.

They get closer and I cast a glance at the third man. He's as tall as the first but other than being a solid mountain of muscle, he's opposite in every other way. Short dark hair, dark complexion, and five-day-old stubble covering his hard-set jaw. The face he's wearing isn't angry, it's pure rage. My gut sinks. I'll go down fighting today but unless these guys show me mercy, I won't be walking out of here. I might be lucky to be left alive.

I resist the urge to turn my head, my eyes desperate for one last look at the girl who is the beginning of my end. As much as I want that final glance, I can't give these brutes more of an advantage than they already have. I keep my eyes on them, every muscle in my body tense. The first one gets within striking distance but I don't move. I *will* fight back but not until one of them makes the first move. "Keela." The sound rumbles from his barrel chest, his focus not on me but burning through the couple behind me. I take a step forward and the whole world grows dim, the noise in my head quieting into an unsettling silence while each beat of my heart is slower than the last. Everything is still. Frozen in place. Everything except for the men. The first one blows past me and I try to block him but my movements are sluggish, as if I'm encased in wet cement. I flick my eyes to the second man and for the briefest of moments, his ice-blue gaze rakes over me. Then he's gone, following in the footsteps of his twin and leaving the third man to pass through my listless line of sight. This one is wound as tight as I am, his massive biceps threatening to rip through the fabric of his shirt. My arms aren't as big as his and even at my size, it's hard to find shirts with enough bicep room. Not something I should be worrying about right now. If every man here loses a shirt due to an overflexed muscle, that still won't be the worst thing that happened today.

I will my body to move. To follow the stone-faced men. No matter how hard I push, my limbs are stuck in the suddenly thick resistance of the air around me. Inch by brutal inch I force my lethargic body away from the underbrush. Like everything else that's happened since the raven drew my attention to the beautiful girl, I'm left without a rational explanation of what's happening to my own body. I gasp but it feels more like a long, slow inhale as I set my lazy eyes on the beautiful girl leaning casually against the tree her boyfriend's back had just been pressed to. She's alone. He left her here to face these men alone? *Coward.* The beastly voice in my head growls and I feel the pressure in the air around me ease ever so slightly.

The men form a line in front of her. The one with the shaved sides of his head exposed steps forward, crossing his arms. "What in all of Midgard do you think you're doing, sister?"

Sister? Some of the tension in my shoulders relaxes but my muscles are still straining as I try to move forward. I scan the men again. Their postures say they're ticked off but none of them are poised to attack her, though the dark-haired one seems close to it. He's also the only one of the three with any resemblance to her, outside of them all being level ten on a gorgeous scale that stops at nine. A rare feat for an individual, let alone an entire family. Does Merrymont use looks as a factor for admission? Another unimportant thing to think about, considering what's happening right now. At least to me. None of the others seem to be affected by whatever is in the atmosphere that's making it hard for me to blink, let alone take another step.

The now named Keela pushes off the tree, still looking as bored as she did when I first saw her sitting atop the wall. "How kind of you to ask, Gelby," she answers Shaved Head in a soft voice. "Among other things, I'm reminding Rohan that rules are not laws and though I have no problem breaking either, I've done neither today."

"Keela." The deep rumbling voice of the first man cuts through the silence.

"Rohan," she mocks his tone.

He surges forward. "This is not a game!"

She leans into his face. "Isn't it?"

His body goes stiff, the two of them locking in a battle of will, staring at one another, neither of them backing down. The third brother pounds his way toward them but the second removes his arms from his barrel chest and puts his own body between her and the dark-haired one. "Not here, Haldir. We already have one loose end to tie up." His eyes land on mine again and a shiver races through me. I'm the loose end.

Keela shoves past him. "A loose end is better than a loose cannon, and yet I'm surrounded by all of you." She walks directly toward me. That burning sensation I felt earlier starts in my right hand, races up my arm, and branches out from there to infect every part of me. It's intense and uncomfortable, yet oddly pleasant. More than that, I can finally breathe again. I take a lungful of air and smile at her, the need to speak to her its own living thing. "Hi."

She smiles back at me, her amber eyes fixing on mine. My insides liquefy. Her smile isn't reaching her beautiful eyes but that doesn't stop my heart from wanting to leap out of my chest to implant itself into hers. "I'm Sean." My voice sounds a little breathy. "It's nice to finally meet you. *Really* nice."

Thunderous grunts rumble behind her but I don't care about her brothers. Or her boyfriend. Now that I can finally move again all I want to do is make sure she's okay. I move toward her and she lifts her palm, flattening it to my chest and lowering her eyes to the spot where her fingers are splayed. She tilts her head as if she can hear the beat of my heart. It was frantic a moment ago and now it's euphoric. Her eyes lift to mine, that insincere smile fading as quickly as it had spread across her lips. I cover her hand with my own. She yanks her palm from my chest. "Go home, Sean. The last thing you remember is speaking to Collin MacKenzie at the student center. After that, you went home."

A sensation akin to ants crawling underneath my skin skitters along my scalp, marching down my spine, and exiting through my toes. "Home," I repeat, lowering my eyes from hers. I turn away, pick up my discarded duffle bag, and follow the path back out of the woods.

Sunlight warms my face as I emerge from the darkness of the trees. I turn right and walk along the wall, casting a glance over the staff parking lot. My left hand begins to itch. I absently rub at it, the friction causing the itch to flare into a burning sensation. I hook my bag on my shoulder and lift the itching hand, expecting to find an insect bite but there's no mark. There isn't even any redness. Yet the burning continues to spread, as if it's inside my veins and circulating with each pump of my heart.

I lean my back against the fence and examine my hand more closely. Something had to have bitten me. Or I walked through a patch of poison ivy while I was in the woods. I look to the end of the fence where I emerged from the path. Why was I back there? The last thing I remember is talking to Collin, and now I'm here. I'm supposed to be going somewhere, though. *Home.* My dorm? Or Collin's frat house? I can't get to either of them from this location, so why would I come this way?

I scratch at my hand. Maybe I could think straight enough to remember why I'm back here on the edge of campus if this infuriating burning would stop. A flash of black hair catches my attention. It emerges from the woods in the exact same spot I did and turns toward the back of the library. I lower my hands and watch the pale-skinned girl stroll across the parking lot. Now *there's* a good reason to be back here. I'll consider my momentary amnesia serendipitous.

I push off the wall and jog across the parking lot, keeping my eyes fixed on the captivating girl gliding over the pavement ahead of me. Everything about Keela works for me. From her deliciously delicate body to those painted-on jeans. Wait. How do I know her name? I slow my pace, keeping distance between us as I rack my brain for the moment in time when I could have met her. With the way she looks and a name like Keela, there's just no way I would forget her. I could have met her at a bar and she gave me a fake name, but even so, her face is the kind of masterpiece that would have stuck with me. So why can't I recall any memories of her?

She steps onto the sidewalk near the library. I slow my pace a little more and follow her, moving onto the sidewalk a safe distance behind her while I continue to tug on every corner of my brain for the spot holding her memory. I can't approach her until I figure out where I met her because if I know her name, she probably knows mine. Meaning I can't walk up and introduce myself as if we're total strangers. You only get one shot with a girl like that and I'm starting to think I might have already had mine.

I check my hand. The last thing I need is to be itching like I have chiggers when I finally get to speak to her...again, apparently. The burning is subsiding, though. The back of my hand is still a little itchy, as if something is sitting just under my skin, making me want to scratch at it until it's unearthed. A tempting thought considering how annoying the itch is, but I'm going to take a wild guess and say that a woman would rather you be scratching when you walk up to her than have a bloody hole in your hand, and right now, Keela is my priority. She's too tempting for me to lose sight of.

I lower my hand and look up just as Keela rounds the side of the library. I pick up my pace and make each step count as I hasten to the corner of the building, skirting around the side of the library only to spot her thick mass of dark hair trotting down the steps that flow along the far side of the patio that interlocks with the one in front of the student center. I hang back and watch her. She veers off onto the sidewalk leading to the walkway by the road, moving as if she's in no hurry to be any place in particular, but making quick work of exiting campus grounds all the same. Odd, since she just got here. Maybe cutting through campus is a shortcut to get from where she was to where she's going. Maybe she isn't a student here, but a local. In which case, my chances of seeing her again are considerably less. No part of me is okay with that. In fact, the very idea of never seeing her again makes my stomach churn. I kick my feet into gear and run down the stairs. Without a doubt, the closer I get to her, the less I feel like cutting off my hand.

4

I've only been black-out drunk one time and I was at Collin's house when it happened. I highly doubt I met Keela then. Collin would have told me about the hot girl I hooked up with, whether I was successful at it or not. So what line could I have approached Keela with that wouldn't make it obvious that I don't remember her? *Hey, what's up?* Lame. It might have been my safest bet, though. Now, it's too late. I kept my stupid mouth shut, trailing far enough behind her not to seem like I was outright following her while shamefully matching every step she took. If I'd only followed her just off campus and then stopped, I probably wouldn't despise myself right now. That's not what I did, though. I followed her down every street, making all the same turns until we ended up in this wealthy-looking neighborhood. It isn't gated, but neither is the estate where Collin lives, and his family is loaded.

I swipe a hand over my sweat-soaked brow. While I tailed Keela, contemplating what I should say to her, I didn't plan on her disappearing behind the colossal two-door entrance of a stately white-sided house. I scan the red brick columns holding up the roof of its porch. When she first entered this residential area, I paid no attention to the mix of older homes. I was too busy nursing a headache over the fact that I was eventually going to have to man up and approach her without having a single clue as to how I know her. Then she turned into the yard of this large home and strolled up the stone walkway. I planted my feet, expecting her to knock on the massive doors. Instead, she marched up the steps, flung open the door on the right, and slammed it unceremoniously behind her. I hadn't even known she was angry until the thwack of the slamming door reached my ears. Did she know I was following her?

I look around me. One of the neighbors has probably spotted me standing out here on the edge of the street like a stalker by now. So much for my sterling reputation. I'd rather knock down all of my professors than get arrested for being a creep. Especially since this could have been avoided if I'd just worked up the nerve to speak to Keela. Admitting that I'm foggy on the details of how I know her and hearing her tell me to get lost would have been crushing, but better than feeling so uncertain about where I stand with her. I don't even know why I care so much about what she thinks of me. I've never been in love before. Of that I'm sure. So why is my head screaming that Keela is mine? Why is my heart answering with affirming thuds, tattooing her name across its surface and her face along every inch of my chest?

I dry my sweaty hands on my jeans and look around one more time. Some of the homes here are much smaller than Keela's but they make up for their size with lavishly landscaped yards that would be more appropriately called gardens. I'm sure they require a lot of tending to, but thankfully for me, I don't see anyone out and about. The whole neighborhood is quiet. Except for the raven preening itself in the neighbor's tree. I'm probably being paranoid but I swear it's the same one that tried to nest in my hair this morning. I keep an eye on it as I cross the street and begin to walk up the stone path. Unlike the smaller homes around this three-story estate, Keela's place has minimal landscaping. Still, every inch of the lawn is meticulous. There are tall pines dotted around the yard, obscuring part of the house as the row of pines closest to the home grow tighter and thicker in number. It's the kind of simple landscaping that will look like a winter wonderland once the snow begins to fall.

I walk up the wide steps that are designed from the same red brick that forms the porch's columns. I've never been so nervous to speak to a woman before, especially one that I've apparently already had some sort of interaction with. I don't even think I've ever experienced anxiety before, and now it's out of control. Not only will I have to admit that I had the audacity to forget about her, but I'll have to confess to having followed her from campus. By some miracle, maybe she'll be willing to overlook today's inexcusable actions and allow me to make up for whatever it is I might have done in the past. She doesn't look like the type of woman who will tell me to get lost. She looks sweet. Kind. Fragile, even. The type of woman who makes a man want to hold her tight and lift her up because even a sad turn to her lips will bring your whole world crumbling down around you. The type of woman a man doesn't forget about. So how in the heck did I let her slip my mind?

I stand in front of the two doors that stretch all the way up to about ten feet in height. The dark wood is weathered and worn, yet it still exudes an air of elegance. This home was built to last. The kind of place meant to stand against time for generations to come. It's too nice to be a rental home connected to the college, which means it's most likely Keela's family home. Especially since her brothers showed up in the woods. Wait. Her brothers?Is that why I was on the edge of campus today? Are Keela's brothers in Sigma Beta Λύκος?

"Darn you, Collin," I curse him and his hazing buddies under my breath as I lift my hand to the door on the right. I don't see a doorbell so I knock, taking out my frustration with Collin and his frat brothers on the hard plank of wood. It swings open. Not much. Just enough to give me a glimpse of the entryway. "Hello?" I call out. No one responds. The inside of the house is quiet. Eerily so. I press my finger against the wood and push the door open a little farther. I didn't notice the recoil when Keela slammed it earlier, but instead of the latch catching, the door must have banged off the frame.

I study what I can see of the inside of the silent home. Directly in front of me is a red-tiled entryway. Beyond that, a wide staircase spills down into what looks like a formal living room that stretches off to the right. Behind the staircase and fanning out to the left is a large octagonal room with ceilings taller than what I can see from my spot on the porch. I move a little closer to the threshold. Around the second-story level of the octagonal room is a balcony. I wonder if Keela swept up the steps when she entered the house and now she's up there watching me, silent as a mouse because she's afraid of the creepy guy who followed her home. I clear my throat and step just inside the door. "Hello? Keela? It's Sean Winkle. Can we talk?"

I wait for her response, or any sound at all for that matter, but the house isn't only silent, it has an empty feeling to it. If Keela *did* know I was following her, she could have run through the house and exited out a back door. She could be at a neighbor's house calling the police right now. Which means I should turn around and go back outside, but instead, I take two more steps across the tiled entryway. Breaking and entering will go well with the other charges I'm racking up today. Though, technically, I didn't break in. The door was open.

"Keela?" I call out to her in what I hope is a soothing tone. "I saw you at Merrymont today." *And I've been stalking you ever since.* "I thought we should talk and I noticed your front door is open. Are you okay in here?"

My words aren't exactly doing me any favors but if she's in here hiding, freaked out because I followed her, I need to at least try to calm her down. Putting eyes on her again will definitely calm my own nerves down. I don't want her to be afraid of me. I want her to love me. I close my eyes to the truth of that thought. What on earth is wrong with me?

I open my eyes. Despite the disgust tightening my stomach into a knot, I continue to walk carefully through the house, fully aware that each step I take is only tightening the noose around my neck. My parents raised me better than this and the last thing I ever want to do is disappoint them, but my desire to speak to Keela is greater than the urge to turn around. Her brothers might have done something to haze me for the fraternity, and once they find out I've trespassed in their home because I'm suddenly infatuated with their sister what they do to me is going to be much worse than whatever it was that they did to give me temporary amnesia, but I still need to talk to her. My quivering, burning, aching insides are demanding it. "Please, Keela, will you talk to me? I'm not going to hurt you. I swear."

I move toward the stairs. There's ivy trailing up the railing and fanning out along the balcony like tinsel. Foggy snapshots of what happened in the woods today play in front of my eyes as I walk deeper into the home. I see Keela's three brothers and a white-haired guy with painted nails who is smiling at me. Now his mouth is on Keela's. My head explodes, thunder filling the space inside my skull. My breath comes out in shallow spurts and the images in my head become clear. Keela *willingly* kissing him. Her musclebound brothers storming onto the scene and her boyfriend fleeing while my entire body was stuck in air thick as glue. Why couldn't I move?

The icy gaze of her second brother, Gelby, flashes before me. I don't know how, but he's the one who did that to me. He made it impossible for me to get to her. "Keela?" I shout this time, rage coiling in my belly as I stomp past potted plants, highly polished dark wood furniture, and neutral-colored walls. The heavy drapes pulled back to the edges of all of the windows are green, all of the carpets a mix of reds, greens, and golds. Outside of that, the only other thing bringing this home to life is the artwork. There are no family portraits that I can see, or even shoes by the front door. I pause at the bottom of the stairs. Instead of going up, my gut tells me to keep walking.

I move forward, entering the octagonal room. It's larger than what it originally appeared. Larger even than what the whole house appears to be capable of containing. This must be the part of the house that the towering pines outside are obscuring. Off to the right, after passing underneath the balcony, there's a dining room with a long dark wood table flanked by fifteen ornately carved chairs. The center is set with greenery and candles. I look up to the balcony that curves around most of the room. My breath catches at the sight of the domed ceiling towering three floors above me. The center is glass, the triangular panes fitted between thick gold seals that flow down to a brightly painted mural of beasts hiding in forests. Dragons, giants, and sea serpents. The stuff of children's stories turned into the most stunning adornment I can imagine.

I study the painting. The most magnificent part of the whole mural is the eight-legged horse flying across a sunsetting sky. I stare at the scene for a minute longer, all manner of new creatures popping out the more I look at the mural. Tiny blue beings forming clouds on the left, and a mermaid lifting from a pool of water at the bottom of the triangle farthest from me. It's captivating. But I'm not risking jail time to gawk at artwork. I'm here for one reason only. I need to find the girl who is stirring something much more dangerous than jealousy inside of me. This itching inferno blazing through my veins has everything to do with her. So does the rage sitting idly by, ready to strike at anyone who stands in between us. It's *my* lips she should have been kissing today. I have no idea how I'll prove that to her but there's not a cell in my body that isn't up for this challenge. "Keela," I call her name again. With my memories coming back, I now know today was my first glimpse of her. That makes it even more odd to be so enraged by jealousy. Keela feels like my home, though. The place I belong. "You're safe with me," I offer, wishing Mom was still here so I could ask her for advice on how to go about this. Trespassing certainly isn't the way to win a girl's heart.

Despite what little knowledge I have of love, I know for a fact that jealousy isn't part of it. My parents always told me trust is the most important thing. That if you can't trust the people in your life, you shouldn't have relationships with them because the people closest to you are the ones who will make or break your life. I guess that's why Collin and I always stuck together. His family doesn't welcome too many outsiders but me punching him forged a bond between the two of us. Ever since that day, we've each had complete trust in each other. My relationship with him doesn't help me in this situation with Keela, though, and for as many times as I heard my parents tell their love story, buying into the whole *when you know, you know* spiel, they never once mentioned that *knowing* you'd found the one would also mean feeling as if your skin is on fire. Or like you want to disembowel anyone who gets close to your partner.

I walk toward the ornate fireplace. Between the heat of the day and my frazzled nerves, I'm a ball of sweat. I need a shower. Or, at the very least, an extra dose of deodorant. Maybe even a comb and a bottle of gel. All things I'm not going to get before seeing Keela because I'm not capable of rational thought right now, as evidenced by the fact that I can't even convince myself to go back to stand on the front porch like a normal person.

I scan the large stone planters nestled on either end of the fireplace's wide hearth. The mantel is made of similar stone and it's decorated much the same way as the dining room table. Greenery and candles. No family photos. I really wish there was something in this house that didn't reek of formality because even the pompous Mackenzie family is casual. Their estate backs up to thousands of acres of national forest and the main home on their land is an eight thousand square foot over-the-top mansion. The inside of the house is loud, though. People are always coming and going. Collin is the second oldest of eight siblings and even cousins of his are regularly milling about. Some of them live in the guest houses scattered along the edge of woods on the estate. I've not been inside all of the cottages but the ones I have walked into look much the same as the main house. Strewn with clothes, blankets, books, and the occasional pizza box. Not the kind of messy that's disgusting, but in the way that makes it very clear that people live there. The kind of people who like to eat, shop, and horseplay. In Keela's house, nothing is out of place, and not a single thing is stirring. Not even a mouse.

I lean closer to the mantel. There are markings on the face of the thick slab of stone, something like the characters of the Japanese language. I run my hand over the symbols. With a moan, the fireplace entrance shimmers and...grows, opening up wide like a mouth at the dentist's office.

5

I jump away from the fireplace's gaping maw. In the blink of an eye, it shrinks back to its original size. I study the stone mantel and the bricks of the fireplace itself. Nothing is broken or cracked. I squeeze my eyes shut and then open them again, staring at the impossibility. There's no way that just happened. I must be dehydrated or something. That's probably why I forgot about meeting Keela and her brothers too. I've had a long and emotional eight months, and walking onto campus as a freshman this morning after enduring such a hard journey to get to Merrymont was overwhelming. I'm drained. Especially now that I've sweated all of the fluid out of my body.

I take a deep breath and press the heels of my hands into my eyes. They're playing tricks on me. I should have gone to my dorm like I told Collin I was going to because then I wouldn't be standing here hallucinating while trying to contain an inner beast I didn't know I was capable of having. I lower my hands and open my eyes. The fireplace is still normal. I cautiously approach it again. I need to prove to myself that I *am* hallucinating because even Gelby being able to slow down my motions today doesn't make any sense. It's impossible.

I reach out and rest my hand on the stone mantel. Nothing happens. I exhale the breath trapped in my lungs. *See, Sean? All normal.* I move my palm across the symbols and with a yawn, the mouth of the fireplace gapes open again. I yank my hand away but the mouth continues to open. It groans and creaks, the top of the opening growing higher than the top of my head. I stumble away from it, peering into the darkness that has to be at least eight feet tall and wide enough to drive a small car through. "No. Way." I slap myself. My cheek stings, and there's still a cave entrance in front of me.

I glance behind me. The house is still quiet. Is this why? Keela is in there, wherever *there* is. I rub my eyes again. I'd rather see Keela or her brothers behind me, laughing over the optical illusion they're fooling me with than be faced with believing this is really happening. "Keela!" I shout into the darkness. There's no response. Not even an echo filtering back to me from the...cave. That has to be what this is. A cave whose opening just happens to be inside this house, concealed by a magic fireplace. I slap myself again. *Magic isn't real.* Whatever is going on here, it isn't magic. I'll find out exactly what it is once I find Keela. If she knew I was following her and wanted to hide from me, this cave would be the perfect place to go. Too bad for her that today is a day of many firsts for me. I stretch my arm out, letting my fingers graze the space inside the opening, extending them until they wholly disappear into the darkness. A coolness bites at my fingertips as if I've just stuck them into a refrigerator. I yank them out and inspect each digit. They're all still attached to my hand.

I move closer to the opening, this time letting the darkness swallow my arm up to my elbow. Once again, I feel a cool draft against my skin. I tug my arm free and turn it over, looking for any sign of damage. Nothing. "Has to be a cave," I mumble, as if saying the words out loud not only makes it true, but somehow negates the fact that for me to even experience this cave, reality as I know it can't exist.

Swallowing my apprehension, I step over the line where the hardwood meets the hearth. There's only one way to prove to myself that any of this is real and to find out whether or not this is where Keela disappeared to. I take another step. Then another. Steadily moving forward, deeper into the cave. The air around me grows colder, the light dimmer, until I'm surrounded by near total darkness. I fill my lungs with the crisp air. It's clear, like being on the shores of Okanagan Lake at the cusp of spring. My parents and I camped there two springs in a row when I was a kid, fulfilling one of my dad's lifelong dreams of seeing British Columbia. Mom loved the location so much that we went back for that second trip and planned a third before ever leaving. Dad died that fall. Mom and I never felt up to going back there without him, choosing instead to have all of our memories of that serene place to be ones that included him.

Forasmuch as the crisp air around me reminds me of Okanagan Lake, the smooth stone walls of the dark corridor are a far cry from the richness of the lake's landscape. Dim orbs hang near the top of the wall, casting shadows along the ceiling. I listen for the echo of my footsteps as I walk but there is none. There's light up ahead, though. And voices. Angry ones. This has to be where Keela fled to.

I keep a steady pace as I move toward the sounds of arguing. There's enough light for me to see the outline of what looks like another cave opening. I slide against the cool stone of the wall, creeping closer to where the corridor I'm in meets with the bright room. I peek around the corner. The room is circular, reminding me of the room where the fireplace exists behind me, only this one is carved from stone. There are hallways jutting off in three other directions, all of them tall and wide, just like the one I'm in now. The room directly in front of me is like a nerve center with all the corridors going out of this one space, but I imagine any college dorm would kill for a common area like this one. It's a cross between a lounge and a games room, with a pool table squarely in the center of the stone floor. The legs of the pool table are resting on a palatial rug of creams and golds. More rugs just like it are scattered here and there, marking each area of the large room as its own space. There's a foosball table, wooden dart board, various plush couches and chairs, and a video game console with one of the largest televisions I've ever seen hanging on the wall.

I take in everything before me, wishing the décor was the strangest thing my eyes were beholding inside this cave, but it's not even close. Keela is standing on the far side of the pool table, the dark-haired third brother from the woods beside her, staring at her profile from only an inch away as angry words growl out of him. Those words aren't the only thing coming out of him, though. Tendrils of smoke are curling out of his nostrils. They spread between his nose and her cheek before rising to disappear into the air above her head. "Aether is Unseelie, Keela."

She wipes the condensation off her face and walks away from him. "He's Seelie, Haldir, and I'll remind you and Rohan both that Aether and I have broken no laws."

A snort comes from behind the big beanbag chair in front of the gaming console. The second brother, Gelby, pops his ponytailed head over the top. "No technical laws, but loads of rules, so Hal and Rohan are only trying to remind you that the Fae don't know the difference between rules and laws."

She lifts a pool stick off the table and points it at him. "Exactly why someone should teach them the difference."

"Enough!" booms a voice from a corner where Rohan is sharpening a sword. A very long and sharp-looking one. His ice-blue eyes match Gelby's, and they're as intent on Keela as Haldir's are, only Rohan doesn't have smoke wafting out of his nostrils. He stands from the chair he's perched on, holding the sword at his side. "Aether is a Seelie prince bonded to the Unseelie and bound to betray them as every other bonded Fae before him has done. He will *not* choose you. Ever."

She throws the stick at Rohan as if it's a spear. His eyes flare orange and he meets the spear with his sword. The wooden stick splinters, splitting in two as it slices along his blade, the two pieces clanging against the floor in front of him. Keela's hands ball into fists. "*No one* will ever choose me. That's what you meant to say, *brother*. Not the Fae, not—" Her head snaps around, eyes homing in on my peeking head. "Human."

Haldir and Rohan snap their eyes to mine the same way Keela just did. Gelby vaults over the back of his chair, glaring at me. *Crap.* I shove off the wall and run, heading back down the corridor and praying the fireplace hasn't shrunk back to normal size. Coward or not, I don't want to be trapped in Alice's hole to Wonderland with...with...whatever those people are. My left hand ignites and the thunder in my head threatens to buckle my knees. My body wants nothing more than to return to Keela but my home or not, she's going to have to wait until I figure out what in the hell is going on.

I toss my duffle bag from my shoulder. My whole life is inside of it but I'm barely able to keep my feet under me, I don't need the extra weight dragging me down. I pump my legs and keep my eyes on the corridor ahead of me. Whatever reason my body has for reacting to Keela, it'll have to wait. She's surrounded by freak shows and I can't go up against them until I know what in the heck they are. The beast in my head roars his disagreement but my survival skills are stronger than his murderous intentions. I slam through the unseen barrier, finding myself once again surrounded by the octagonal room. My forward momentum carries me too far and I leap over the slender coffee table, my foot catching on the back of the leather sofa as I attempt to clear them both. My body slams into the hardwood floor. Air rushes out of my lungs and I fight to get it back as I shove upright, scrambling for the door as fast as I can. There's no looking back to see how close anyone is or to check whether the fireplace is back to normal or still gaping open. I want to survive, so I'm not sparing a single second.

I race through the house and spill out into the late August heat, jumping from the porch and sticking a biting landing on the stone pathway. Pain shoots up my legs but I keep my feet moving. I run for the road. A bright light flashes in front of me, growing wide and oval, the edges crusted with what looks like lightning. The attractive white-haired guy Keela kissed in the woods leaps out of the light, his arm outstretched. I try to avoid the punch but we're both moving too fast. He shoves his fist into my chest. Electricity explodes inside me. The burning in my hand is nothing compared to the pain of being cooked from the inside out. My back arches. I yell but the sound burns away in my throat. Another light bursts across my vision. Then the whole world goes dark.

6

"How did he get inside?" A man's voice filters through the void around me. I try to find him but I'm floating in nothingness, my spirit detached from my physical body and surrounded not by darkness, but by nothing. A pain jabs between my eyes. Poking. Digging. I pull away from it and bright blue vines of electricity burst across the void, skimming over the nothingness around me, eating up the space and replacing the nothingness with sizzling light.

Keela's face flashes between the vines. I see her sitting on the wall in front of the student center, walking into the woods, kissing someone who isn't me, and looking at me with golden-hued amber eyes, telling me to forget, to go home.

"We have no idea, Bishop." Another voice reaches inside the nothingness. One I recognize. This is the brother called Gelby. I follow his voice, stretching my arms out toward the sizzling blue vines cocooning around me. "I've checked him twice. He has no magical signature. As far as I can tell, he's human."

"Which doesn't explain how he fought off Keela's compulsion." Another voice. The brother called Rohan. "We all heard her compel him, and we all saw him leave."

Compulsion? I roll the word around in my head. The first voice I heard answers Rohan with a low hum. "Yet he crossed into our world. Alone. Keela, do you have an explanation?"

"No, Bishop," she answers. My body seizes at the sound of her voice. I bite down, a wave of panic washing over me as I fail to control the convulsions fitfully racing through my body. "When he followed me, I assumed it was only because the human lived nearby. I didn't think he was actually *following* me."

A growl rattles my abyss and my seizing body begins to calm, instead growing hot as the vines surrounding me shudder and fade. I wish I didn't, but I know exactly who, or *what*, this growl belongs to. Haldir. The boy with the smoking nostrils. "That's because you don't think at all, Keela. If you hadn't broken Bishop's orders just to hook up with Aether, none of this would be happening."

Another growl makes the now mellow vines vibrate. This one female. When she speaks, instead of seizing again, I start to see light spreading through the nothingness. "I wasn't *hooking up* with anyone. I was meeting with Aether because he said he had important news. The kiss was for the human's benefit. He followed me from campus and since Aether was waiting for me, I made a call on how to handle him that allowed me to *follow* Bishop's rules of not using my power unnecessarily."

"You *handling* people is why we're in this mess," Rohan says, his cold tone sending an icy shudder through my soul. "This isn't the first time you and Aether have insisted upon playing your little games, and now look at what that has brought us. More trouble."

"I didn't bring the human here!" she shouts. The blue vines explode and I scream, the force of the explosion thrusting my weightless spirit downward. I spin and flail, hurtling fast and hard into endless freefall.

"Not on purpose," Bishop says calmly. "There are parts of your power you aren't in control of, though, and because of that, you must use care at all times."

"Yes, Bishop," she mutters.

Despite my fear, warmth spreads through me at the tenderness in his voice when he speaks to her. "I know you do, dear. Which leaves me with only two remaining questions. Who is this boy, and how in all of Yggdrasil's worlds did he get inside this house, let alone through our gateway?"

I slam against something hard, the air knocking from my lungs in a familiar memory. I'm back in my body. I jerk upright, gasping, and barely missing a skull-to-skull collision with Gelby. He smiles. "You're alive. It's a good thing, too. I'd hate to be robbed of the opportunity to kill you myself."

"Gelby!" Four voices shout in unison.

He shrugs. "Keela can just comp... Oops, my bad."

I blink at him. *Compel.* He was going to say that Keela could compel me to forget all of this, but how is that possible? How can she erase my memory with nothing more than her words? This can't be happening. None of it. I cast a frantic glance around the room. I'm in the formal living room at the front of the house. The one I passed by on my way inside when I first arrived. Rohan is straight across from me, along the wall. Smoke-nose is on my right, Keela slightly behind him, and a man as tall as Rohan standing beside her. His belly is round, his cheeks rosy, and his curly white hair matches that of his long, shiny beard. I follow the tips of it down to where it tickles the top of his round belly. *Santa Claus?*

I drop my head and rub it. I must have hit it. That's what happening. Collin probably ended up tackling me because he thinks roughhousing is appropriate anywhere, and I'm currently conked out on the lawn of Merrymont, having the most vividly detailed hallucination ever.

Black boots step into my line of sight. I look up. Santa bends over, propping his hands on his knees, a twinkle in his eye. They're blue, just like Rohan's and Gelby's. "Hey there, young man." I can see the smile in those eyes but not on his face because it's covered by fluffy white Santa Claus hair. "You had a nasty fall outside. The stone on our sidewalk can get quite slick."

I run my hands up through my hair, fisting it and tugging at my scalp. If I fell here, was it before or after I walked into a fireplace? *Santa. Fireplaces.* My gut somersaults. "Yeah, I fell."

"Outside of our home," Haldir growls. I glance at him. His arms are folded over his chest but there's no smoke escaping his nostrils. He looks normal. A little unnaturally large, but steroids can do that to a body. Maybe he's one of those kinds of idiots.

"Yeah, I fell. Outside." I answer how I think I'm supposed to. Anything to wake up from this nightmare. I only wish I could take Keela into reality with me. My gaze flits to hers.

Haldir's hulking form steps in front of her. "Why did you come here?"

Keela moves to the side, watching me over his shoulder. I lock eyes with her and smile. "Isn't it obvious?"

Haldir looks behind him and drops his arms with an irritated sigh. "No, it isn't obvious." He steps toward me, once again blocking Keela from my view. "Explain why you came here. Without lying, because we'll know if you lie."

I look away from him and stretch out my legs. If this isn't real, I should just ignore him. I glance at the door. If I get up and walk out of here, will I wake up? Rohan steps in front of the door. "You may have entered our home uninvited but you will not leave it until we're done with you. How quickly that happens depends on you."

I scan the five faces around me. Rohan. Santa. Gelby. Haldir. And Keela, who is once again off to the side of Haldir's shoulder, looking at me indifferently. "Do you feel it?" I ask her.

Her eyes narrow but it's Haldir who speaks. "She feels nothing for you, human." To her he says. "Go check in with Siohma. She'll need your help preparing dinner."

Her narrow gaze turns on him. "Bite me, Hal."

He turns in her direction. "Only if you bite me back."

"Enough," Rohan barks at them. "Bishop will issue the orders, Haldir. And you've caused enough trouble for one day, Keela. The only thing you'll be biting for the rest of the day is your tongue."

She crosses the room. I watch her, as captivated now as I was when I saw her sitting on the wall outside the student center. Only there's no burning sensation inside of me now. No warmth. Not even a tiny itch. More importantly, there's no beastly voice in my head urging me to conquer the world for her. She stands tall in front of Rohan. "I was *not* the cause of what happened today. Blame me all you want but doing so will not change the truth."

His stare hardens to stone. "What truth would that be, *sister?*"

She presses a finger into his chest. "That I am not afraid of you any more than I'm afraid of Aether's family. His blood, his bond, they all care for him about as much as all of you care for me."

"Keela," Santa says her name with a mix of tenderness and concern.

She spins away from Rohan and meets no other eyes in the room but mine. She walks to me and drops to her knees in front of me. "May I ask you some questions?"

I reach forward and touch her face. She feels so real. So soft. "Ask me anything."

Gelby slaps my hand away from her and I glare at him. "This is my dream, get your own."

Santa chuckles and I can't help but watch his belly jiggle like a bowl full of jelly. Soft hands curl over my knees, drawing my attention back to Keela, who is still on her own knees in front of me. I so want to be alone with her. She rises up enough to look into my eyes. "What do you remember about what happened to you today?"

My hands twitch, every instinct I have telling me to grab her beautiful face and kiss her. But her boyfriend did that already. Then he shoved his fist inside my chest. The memory slams into my head and my hand leaps to my chest, patting at my sternum and running over every inch of my pecs. There's no hole. I look down at my shirt. No blood. "It's all a dream. I hit my head and all of this is a dream."

"Is that all you remember?" Keela asks. "Hitting your head outside our home?"

My mouth goes dry. "I, um...no." I don't want to lie to her but something is telling me that hallucination or not, I need to get out of here as quickly as possible.

She smiles at me. "Tell me everything you remember about today, Sean. Starting with your arrival at Merrymont University."

The ants I felt crawl over my scalp when I was in the woods with her are back. But this time, they reach the back of my head and disappear. Is her compulsion not working on me again? And why does all of this feel so real? So scary? "Um, I met my friend Collin at the student center. Then I saw you." She knows this much already. Apparently. "I wanted to introduce myself so I followed you." I shake my head as if the rest of the memory is fuzzy. "Then, I don't know. I just sold my house and I haven't moved into my dorm. My friend wanted me to move into his fraternity house anyway, so I...I think I got lost."

She lifts a brow. "That explains some things. You were lost and followed me because you currently have no home, and I was all that was familiar to you." She cups my face and gets closer to me, her pupils dilating and rimming in thick gold bands. "I'm no longer familiar to you. You've never seen me before and if you see me later, you'll have no interest in me whatsoever. I'm only another face in the crowd. Gelby is your friend, though. He's helping you get settled at college. You trust him." Her eyes dim and she peers at her fingers, then back at me once more before ripping her hands from my face and regaining her feet. She straightens and faces Rohan. "Yes, I'll choose my words more carefully next time, but remember that I wouldn't have had to choose *any* if you hadn't shown up. Aether had every right to call me and if he does so again, I'll meet him. Every. Single. Time."

She storms away. Rohan follows her. So does Haldir, and so does Santa...Bishop, whatever the jolly old soul's name is. Gelby stretches his hand down to me. "You look like you need some air, bro. I do, too. Let's take a walk. It's getting ready to get a little noisy around here."

7

Gelby

Eventide has always been my favorite. That point where the darkness meets the light and all nocturnal things begin to wake. It's the same in Alfheim as it is here in Midgard, though I much prefer the dramatics of this human realm to the politics of Alfheim. For that reason alone, I'm glad to be the second son. Rohan has no choice but to return home anytime Bishop calls for him. It is his duty as heir to be at our father's side. It is my duty to oversee our work here in Midgard. Doing so requires constant dedication to enhancing my magic. All Álfar have magic and my lineage is stronger than most, but no Álfr before me has wielded the power as I have.

Bishop says it is enough that all the worlds of Yggdrasil know the strength of the Vasilis line. For them to fear Odin's chosen protectors of Midgard. I remember the great wars, though. Centuries have passed but I've never forgotten the uprising. The All-father himself might have blessed us but I remain vigilant. The Fae will never again rise against my people, let alone stand any chance of slaughtering us as they did before. This is why I warded Keela. Her friendship with Aether may be innocent enough but anytime he is near her, I will know, and my brothers and I will intervene.

I wish Keela would understand why but she wasn't with us during the wars. She didn't see the carnage. The destruction. She was alone in exile. On the day Bishop found her, he took pity on the Vampir and brought her home to us. Since then, she has fought loyally at our side, but she has no memory of her life before exile. She has no knowledge of family outside of us. As well acquainted with death as my sister is, she has not had to look into the eyes of her own mother and watch that life drain away.

Sean Winkle is not Fae, though. I move deeper into the shadows at the edge of his dorm, watching every person entering and exiting the building. My face is well-known to the students at Merrymont. While the school does accept the occasional human, as they've done with this Sean Winkle, most of the students here are young offspring of the many factions of races my family has authority over. Midgard is the human realm and anyone entering from any other world falls subject to our rule. The Vasilis are enforcers, and my sister is one of the best. There are so few of her kind that she's feared simply because she is unknown. She's also ruthless. Many decades have passed since we've had to restrain her but still, stories are whispered among families. I'm hoping to hear a new story tonight. One that tells me why I had to use so much force to put a human male to sleep. There's not a single remarkable thing about Sean Winkle and yet he resisted my magic in the woods, fought off Keela's compulsion, broke through the wards on our home, and somehow wielded enough magic to step into the pocket world my ancestors created thousands of years ago. Never in the recorded history of my people has a human ever crossed into our world.

Keela saw the boy talking to Collin MacKenzie, and she and Haldir both smelled the wolf's lingering scent. Keela's keen senses picked up on other Ulfr, too. Collin's older sister Leah and one of the younger brothers. The Ulfr have no magic beyond that which allows them to shift between human form and wolf, so while they may be the reason Sean Winkle came to Merrymont, they are not capable of imbuing him with power. The most they can do is turn him into one of them. Which still poses no threat to us. The Ulfr fought with us during the wars and while they are notorious for doing only what is best for their pack, meaning they would have turned on us if they thought doing so would benefit them, one Álfr is worth five Ulfr. And that's on an off day. The Ulfr cannot stand against us on their own so if they have something to do with how the human repelled my magic, the wolves are not scheming alone.

A bloodcurdling scream draws my attention away from the entrance to the dorm. I take out my phone and message Hal. I'd intended to stand vigil here all night, not only watching for anyone coming and going who could possibly be strong enough to pick a fight with us, but to protect the kid. I put a ward on Sean's door so if anyone opened it, I'd know. It's the least I can do after having to zap him with powerful magic. I needed him to sleep while I searched his room and the boy didn't go down easily.

As a general rule, we don't use our magic on humans unless absolutely necessary. Sean Winkle made it more than necessary today. *Watch over the boy,* I text Haldir. He'll still be angry over everything that happened earlier but the dragon will come. Dreki are even more rare than Vampir and Hal has been a part of our family longer than Keela. Bishop has a habit of bringing home strays and Haldir was orphaned in the war. He was very small when he came to live with us and after losing so many family members, Rohan and I adopted Haldir as our brother.

We adopted Keela as one of us, too. She was already fully grown and incredibly strong even near starvation, so no one knows how old she truly is. To us, she was just a scared little girl. We all felt compelled to protect her but none more than Haldir. His Dreki nature drove him to guard her as if she was his golden treasure. By the time we realized the full extent of her power, it was too late. She was one of us, and none of us would let her go.

I cut through the lawn and cross over a patio, heading in the direction of the scream. My job isn't to police every fight in Midgard. If the Vasilis get involved, someone has broken a treaty or brought harm to humans. That's why we discourage the elders of Merrymont from admitting humans. They're too vulnerable here among all the others. Those with clout, such as the MacKenzie pack, like to throw their weight around and convince the elders to admit their pet humans. It never ends well.

A wolf races from the tree line, moving so fast its paws barely touch the grass as it speeds off in the same direction I'm headed. "Figures," I mutter. The wolves are loud and obnoxious, and we've had to put them in their place more than once. They're entertaining, though.

I let my magic seep into the air around me. It sizzles and pops along my arms, coating my skin as I begin to search for the wolf's signature.

I can already guess where it's heading. I run toward the direction of the screaming I heard earlier, stopping short when I round the student center. Three young witches are using their magic to subdue a Draugr while the wolf circles it, nipping at the undead creature's limbs, trying to reach its neck without getting caught in the Draugr's crushing grip. They're doing a passable job and I'd be inclined to sit back and watch them continue their battle, but Draugr are not permitted in Midgard. Not the one the girls have managed to knock down with their magic, or the one lumbering up behind them.

The wolf spots the second Draugr and bravely charges it. The witch with the long red braid screams for help. "We can't hold it much longer!" I form my magic into a sharp point and send a flaming blue dagger straight into their Draugr's heart. The creature topples over and I rush forward, whipping my magic into a long blade. I flip overtop the creature's shoulders and slice the sharp edge of my magic through its neck. Its decaying head rolls across the ground, bouncing over the bare feet of the witch with short red hair tamed into a mohawk. She doesn't bother to move away from it. She's too busy gaping at me, the same as the others. Their red hair marks them as Völva, the most powerful coven of their kind. They would each pay handsomely to have magic as strong as mine. I bow to them. "The Vasilis appreciate your assistance. You may go now." I turn and release my magic into dozens of flaming darts. They fly through the air, piercing the body of the second Draugr. The gasps behind me tell me the witches are too enthralled with my display to leave. It's rare for any of them to see a Vasilis in action.

The Draugr stumbles and the wolf pounces, her long body soaring through the air and catching the creature's neck in her powerful jaws. Her head shakes violently and just like that, the excitement is over. The wolf spits out the severed neck and turns to stare at me, her chest heaving and a gleam I know well sparking in her eyes. Battle excites her. As it does me. I give her a nod. "You did well, little wolf."

Her fur begins to change and before I know it, a naked and very attractive Leah MacKenzie is standing in front of me. "We didn't need your help, *little* Vasilis."

A chuckle rumbles through my chest. "Without your pack, not even the witches could help you. Had I not been nearby, you would no longer be so alive, or so lovely."

A deep flush rises in her cheeks as I openly admire her form. She looks behind me. "Leave us."

"But what about the bodies?" one of the witches asks.

I wave them off. "I've already sent word to Alberich. He'll be along for his meal shortly."

Feet slap over the ground and even Leah's eyes shift to the lawn around us. Alberich is more feared than Keela. The Dvergr is the largest and meanest of its kind. Most dwarves are smaller but Alberich is not only massive compared to the others, his diet consists of flesh and bone. As the head of the Vasilis prison, he is the executioner of those we find guilty. Sometimes only after Keela first drains them of their blood. Tonight, Alberich dines on the freshly dead bodies of the undead. I'm not sure how he'll get past the smell but I've seen him eat much worse.

I rake my eyes over Leah again. I need to find out why the Draugr are on campus but I also have other needs and she looks like the woman for the job. "Do you want to go home with me?"

She swallows. "As in…"

I snap my fingers, clothing her in a long dress that's slit up the leg. "As in I'll portal us to a private bedroom, feed you a candlelight dinner, and then remove that dress without using my magic."

A smile spreads across her face and she licks her lips. "Portal us. Remove the dress. Then you can feed me."

I reach out a hand. She slips her palm into mine and I pull her to me. "Your wish is my command."

8

Sean

I roll over, automatically shoving a hand up through my hair before dragging it back down my face. My head is killing me. The pounding is coming from both inside and outside of my skull. Somewhere off in the distance, Collin is shouting. I try to open my eyes but the stabbing pain in my head is nauseating. "Sean! Open the door!" Collin's yell makes it worse. I massage my temples. I don't know what door Collin can't open. He's had a key to my parents' house since we were teenagers. But I just sold that house, didn't I?

I pry one eye open, keeping it squinted against the dim light filtering in through the window across the room. There's a desk underneath that window and my duffle bag is sitting on top of it. I force my second eye open and scan the stark white walls, moving my gaze up to the sea of ceiling tiles above me. Beneath me is a stiff mattress. One devoid of sheets. "Sean!" Collin shouts again, beating on this door he can't open at the same time. "I know you're in there!"

Three sharp bangs punch against the wall next to me. "Shut up!" A female voice screams. "I'm sleeping!"

"Doesn't sound like it!" Collin shouts back at her, still pounding on my door. I push my feet off the end of the bed, fighting against the nausea as I slowly lever the rest of my body up to a sitting position. I scan the room again and this time recognition dawns on me. I've seen pictures of the private dorm room I was lucky enough to land, but how did I get here? And why did I not make my bed?

"Sean!" Collin beats against the door.

"Coming," I yell, wincing as the sound ricochets through my head. Whatever happened to me, this is so much worse than a hangover.

I force myself to stand, bracing for another roll of my stomach. I wish throwing up was the worst of my worries but puking isn't why my body is currently doubling over. I dig my fingers into my scalp. My skull feels like it's on the verge of splitting open. *Keela.* I hear her name as clearly as I hear Collin shouting. I see her face, images of her flitting through my mind so fast it's hard to hold on to any of them. My door cracks, Collin's pounding threating to break it. I stumble in that direction. As my legs move, the images stop, and the pain eases. I lean against the doorframe, wiping my face and feeling the wetness of my tears. "Darn you, Sean!" Collin slams against the door.

I pull up my t-shirt and wipe my eyes. *What in the heck is wrong with me?* As bewildered about the images as I am about how I got into this room and why Collin is currently trying to bust the door down, I yank the slab open. He doesn't give me time to utter a single syllable. He shoulders past me and circles the room. "It's about damn time. What were you doing in here?"

He looks under the bed and I take the opportunity to wipe my face again. I've cried in front of him before. When each of my parents died and even a few times while Mom was sick, but it's not something I do on a regular basis and I don't need him grilling me about why I'm crying when I have no idea why. "Sleeping. And not waking up as easily as everyone else on this floor did."

He smirks. "Yeah, your neighbors are a bunch of witches. Which is why you shouldn't be here. What happened to you yesterday? I looked for you and called your phone for hours. You just disappeared."

I shake my head. The haze around my memories is starting to lift but what I'm remembering isn't possible. I step into the hallway and scan the length of the corridor. My room is on the end closest to the emergency exit. There's a coed bathroom halfway down and beyond that, a main stairwell that leads to the lower three floors. The last thing I remember is walking up those stairs with Gelby. He was talking about video games and I was trying not to freak out as I planned what to do next. If I was dreaming, I needed to wake up. If I wasn't, I needed to run for help.

I duck back into the room. "Did you see—"

Collin flicks my ear. "That my best friend ditched me? Yeah, I noticed that you didn't show up for your own party. What happened to you? I couldn't even track your phone. Did you delete me from your friends list?"

I walk over to my duffle bag and pull my phone from the side pocket. It's dead. I toss it to him and sit on the edge of the bed, dropping my head into my hands. It's not hurting anymore but I wish it were because

I'd rather be in agony than have a memory of meeting Santa Claus last night. "I think I'm losing my mind."

Collin tosses the useless phone onto the bed beside me. "You stood up a houseful of *very* hot women so yeah, you're out of your ever-loving mind. But since you're not dead or dying, there's no time to dwell on you being an idiot. There's someone downstairs who wants to say hello to you, so go take a shower. You smell like you slept in a barn."

I trip over my feet getting off the bed. "Who's downstairs? Keela?"

He stops dead in his tracks. "Keela? You were with Keela Vasilis last night?"

"Vasilis," I mutter. That name doesn't sound right but none of my memories do either. "You know her? Keela is real?"

He grins. "Real, and one heck of a good reason to blow off my party. But do yourself a favor and forget about her. She's a waste of time."

I shake my head at him. "You don't understand—"

"I do," he cuts me off, no longer smiling. "Stay away from her. She's out of your league. Mine, too. And even if she wasn't, she's guarded by three brothers with an attitude problem. If you see any of them again, go in the opposite direction."

I follow him out into the hallway. "You *know* Keela? Not just her name but you know about her family?"

He huffs out a tired breath. "Dude, *everyone* knows her. She's look-don't-touch territory. Even for me, so I'm not being a jerk when I say she's out of your league. Trust me, you have no shot with her, Sean. So shower, get dressed, and don't make me have to come back up here. Your neighbors have attitudes about as terrible as the ones Keela's brothers have."

As much as I'd like to follow him and extract every bit of information he has on Keela and her family, if I go after Collin right now, I'm more likely to end up making him swallow another tooth. I had a crush on his sister Leah for all of five days. She somehow sensed that my thirteen-year-old self was *very* into her fifteen-year-old body, and that's when I learned how brutal the MacKenzie women are. Leah had Collin invite me over to their estate for a pool party. All of the kids from our class and hers were invited. It was a pretty cool party and I was having a blast until the semi-famous pop band she hired began to perform. For two full hours, they played a medley of songs written for, and dedicated to, me. Songs like *No Shot Sean*, which unfortunately had a catchy chorus. Kids sang that song for months on end. Sometimes I still find myself humming the tune.

I stomp back into my room. I have more important things to stew on than Collin or Leah. For starters, I need to seriously consider getting my head examined. Keela is obviously real, but there's no way her father is Santa Claus. I can believe I walked into a magical fireplace more than believe flying sleighs and elves are real. Besides, they called him Bishop, not Santa. So maybe I did follow her home like a psychopath and then I fell on her stone sidewalk, cracked my head, and dreamed the rest.

I unzip my duffle bag. I know I didn't have this with me when Gelby walked me back to campus. The contents all look to be here, though. I shove my clothes aside and pull out the toiletries bag. Grandma's quilt is peeking out from beneath the sheets and my shower sandals are tucked down the sides of the bag how I had them when I packed the bag to begin with. I take them out and rifle through my clothes. I have no idea what is going on but Collin's right about the stench that's clinging to me. The showers are just down the hall so I'll go there and clean up before I...do whatever I can to figure out what happened to me yesterday.

I toss fresh clothes onto the desk beside me and tug off my shirt. I drop it onto the floor, my eyes fixing on the crumpled gray fabric as a memory cuts across my vision. It's of Keela's boyfriend. He's shoving his fist through my chest, cooking me from the inside out. I gulp in air and slap a hand over my chest. It's solid. Firm. Completely devoid of a fist-sized hole. I remove my hand and bounce my pecs to check that my muscles are still working. They are, and I'm not sure how to feel about that. Before the boyfriend, Aether, stepped out of thin air and hit me, I was running from men with smoking nostrils and glowing eyes. Maybe what really happened was instead of falling and hitting my head, Aether spotted me tailing Keela and punched me so hard I bypassed concussion and went straight to brain damage.

I strip off the rest of my clothes, managing to do it without sparking any more asinine memories, and shove the pile of stink into the corner. There are two towels in my bag and I pull out the first one I see, securing it around my waist before tossing my shower sandals onto the floor and stuffing my feet inside. I grab my toiletries. They're in a leather bag with a hook on top. It was my dad's. Mom got it for him the Christmas before he died. I'd forgotten all about it until I was cleaning out her closet and found it tucked into a box with some of his shirts and some old photographs. I kept everything that was in that box. It meant something to her and therefore it means everything to me.

Until this moment, I didn't know how grateful I'd be for Dad's bag, or for the foresight I had when I readied it with the items I'd need to haul back and forth from the communal bathroom. With everything that's going on, if I had to waste time buying soap or even digging through my duffle for a razor, I'd probably be skipping the shower and hating life even more because if I do manage to find Keela today, I'd have to talk to her while smelling like month-old garbage. And I do intend to find her today because whether or not anything else inside of my head is real, she is. Collin just confirmed it and I know with every breath I take that we belong together. The problem is that I don't understand how I know that. I'm hoping she can clue me in, or at the very least tell me she feels the same way I do. If she does, we can figure out the rest. Together.

I head back out into the hallway and make the short trek to the coed bathroom, slipping inside and giving the place a cursory glance. Two girls are off to the left, one of them only in her underwear as she brushes her teeth. I look away. The girl is wearing nothing we wouldn't see on a beach and admittedly, she looks good in her own skin, but Keela is all I can think about. When she looked at me with those gold-ringed amber eyes...it was as if I saw my whole life there. Past. Present. Future. Which is going to be one heck of a problem if the things I'm remembering are true. Especially the compulsion. She tried to make me leave her, forget about her, but it didn't work. Unless that was only for the benefit of her brothers and what she really did was compel me to be in love with her. But why would she? It isn't like she can't get the attention of anyone she wants. Keela's one of those girls who fall into the category of being everyone's type. Besides, I felt all warm and fuzzy inside before she ever even glanced my way. After she looked, that feeling turned volcanic. Then I fell, or was slugged, and proceeded to hallucinate until one of her protective brothers escorted me to my dorm room and left me to sleep off the effects of my concussion. Which is the exact opposite of what a concussed person is supposed to do, but I guess all Gelby cared about was getting rid of me. If he's even real. I managed to fill in the gaps of my memory with visions of jolly old elves and magic fireplaces so he could be another figment of my imagination. The same as his brothers.

I step inside a shower stall and tug the curtain closed before unwrapping my towel and hooking it onto the bottom of the two-pronged hook that's attached to the block wall. I secure my toiletry bag on the top hook and stare at it. It's a *Christmas* gift. Though it's August, I packed this bag only three days ago. That could be why Christmas things jumped into my delusions. "Plausible," I encourage myself. Maybe I'm not losing my mind after all.

I unzip the bag and let it fall open while I turn on the water. It's hot already, which is good. The faster I get this done, the sooner I can go look for Keela. I need answers from her about as badly as I need this shower. I tug the shampoo from its slot and squeeze a dollop into my palm, lathering and scrubbing my hair and body as quickly as possible. "Hey," a female voice calls from outside the stall.

I move under the hot stream and begin to rinse. "Yeah?"

"Are you Sean?" she asks.

I shut off the water and pull my towel off the hook, scrubbing it over my hair. "Yes."

She yanks my curtain open. It's the redhead who was glaring daggers at Collin outside the student center yesterday. This morning, her long braid is curled into a pile on top of her head. "My room is next to yours, so keep the noise down. I had a very long night and if you wake me up ever again, I'm going to cut off your balls and feed them to you."

I tie the towel around my waist. "Message received."

"You better hope so," she snarls, slinging the curtain and storming away. I wait until I hear the sound of the bathroom door opening and closing before I emerge from the stall. I wish Collin wouldn't have shouted my name for the entire dorm to hear. All of my neighbors probably hate me, and that's not going to help my quickly deteriorating reputation. I zip up my toiletry bag and leave the shower stall, moving over to the sinks and avoiding eye contact with the two girls who are still standing there. I'd like to make new friends but so far, I'm only making enemies.

I silently give my teeth a good scrub and then head back out into the hallway, hurrying down the corridor before I have to interact with anyone else. I push the door to my room open and freeze. There's a beautiful woman sprawled across my bed, her high-heeled boots drawing my attention up her legs to where the top of the boots cup her thighs. She swipes her hand over the patchwork quilt, her pointy red nails glistening against the fabric. "I took the liberty of making your bed. Though, from what my brother tells me, you won't be staying in this room." Leah's head cocks sideways, her light brown hair falling over the shoulder her teal-colored shirt is exposing. "You have such striking green eyes, Sean. It's a shame they're what captures my attention most when you're standing in front of me wearing nothing but a towel."

I trudge into my room and toss the bag onto the desk. "Are you the person Collin had waiting downstairs?"

She gets off the bed, her hand running up my arm, over my bare shoulder, and down my back. Her fingernails rake along the length of my spine, all the way down to the top of the towel. "I am, but you were taking too long. I got bored."

I shrug her off of me and pull the t-shirt from the pile of fresh clothes I set aside earlier. I tug it over my head to keep her from fondling my back again. Not that she's doing it because she likes me. She's being arrogant, as usual. But I got over being attracted to her a long time ago so just to prove it, I face her before dropping my towel. Her eyes immediately drop below my waist. The girl who barged into my shower didn't even look. I smile and Leah's teeth snap together. "Modest as ever."

I take my sweet time stepping into my underwear. "If you don't want to see my jewels, then don't break into my room."

She tsks. "We're practically family. Well, we would be if Collin dated boys instead of girls, because he's the only one in the family who truly likes you."

I shove my legs into my jeans. "Then why are you here, sweet cheeks? You dislike me so much that you just had to come make my bed? Or is it the touching you missed? Because for someone who claims not to like me, you sure do put your hands on me every chance you get."

Her lip turns up in a snarl. She hates it when I call her sweet cheeks, which is precisely why I do it. "I'm here because there's been...a situation. One that requires borrowing your boyfriend Collin for a while. I knew me stealing him away from you would hurt, so I wanted to break the sad, sad news to you myself."

I walk across the room, fidgeting with my hair. If I get to see Keela today, I want to look as nice as possible. Since I don't normally do anything to my hair, I have no idea what it needs to constitute *nice*. I glance at Leah. I could ask her, but then I wouldn't trust whatever she tried to talk me into doing. "I've lived with hardly seeing Collin since high school. In fact, since graduation, I've seen you more than him. Now here you are, breaking into my room and pawing at me. Again. I'm starting to believe you want to do more with my jewels than only look at them." I sit on the bed and lean back, as if giving her access to do whatever she wants. "Is that it, sweet cheeks?"

"You wish," she barks, swaying her hips as she sashays to the door. "By the way, Collin is gone already, but he mentioned you had a run-in with Keela." Fury burns in Leah's chocolate eyes. "Stay away from her, or what I do with your jewels will be very, very painful."

9

My run-ins with Leah are never pleasant, but this one was stranger than most. She tends to put her hands on me so that part wasn't completely new, but she only paws at me because she likes being the center of attention and ever since she humiliated me, I've paid her little of that. She isn't the only MacKenzie hankering for the spotlight either. All of them have the same issue. They're competitive, and to Leah, I'm a game. She wants me to want her only so she can humiliate me again. In her mind, it's a power move. So while she probably did come to tell me that she's going to be monopolizing Collin's time because she thinks him not being around will once again ruin the college plans he and I had made, I doubt she'd go through the trouble unless this visit was more self-serving.

I get off the bed and pull the quilt back, checking for thumbtacks or itching powder. If she thought she could ensure my torment, I can see her making my bed. Otherwise, it's too much like kindness, and Leah MacKenzie is anything but kind. I saw the real Leah in the way she said Keela's name. It was hostile, and one of the stranger parts of her visit. Leah *is* the jealous type, but the only way she'd be jealous of someone I'm interested in would be if she thought the girl was of a higher status than herself. She must see Keela as somewhere above her on the societal ladder. Therefore, Leah is warning me off of Keela because my dating someone on a higher rung would mean that I leapfrog over her. That's the way Leah's mind would process it, anyway.

Most wealthy girls in Richlands, where Leah and I are both from, only date guys from other wealthy families. I was always the toy they'd play with, making out with me for fun, but none of them wanted a real relationship with me. For the most part, I was cool with that. I could always get dates when I wanted them and I never wanted to commit myself to a relationship. Collin was the same, and that's another area we bonded over. We truly were only committed to each other growing up. Things change, though. I might be stupid for feeling the way I do, but I'm already committed to Keela. If Leah doesn't like that, she can take a number when it comes to mutilating my genitalia. I'm not sure what's in the water today but I've already had two women threaten to castrate me. I can only hope that Keela isn't drinking from the same well they are.

I grab my truck key from the front pocket of my duffle bag and pick up my dead phone. I'll charge it in the vehicle because classes start tomorrow and I have a mandatory orientation today, but now that Collin is off doing who knows what with Leah, I have no reason to do anything other than visit Keela's house again.

I shove out of my dorm room and head for the stairs, jogging down the flights and pushing out the front doors. It's still fairly early but students are milling about campus, some moving into dorms, others doing yoga or martial arts on various patches of lawn. I pass by a red braid and throw up a friendly hand. The girl only glares at me before going back to reading her book. *Great.* I can go ahead and mark my neighbor off the potential new friend list.

I reach my truck and hop into the driver's seat. Keela made a few turns yesterday but I think I can find her neighborhood again. If all else fails, I'll drive down every street in a ten-mile radius of campus because going back there is important. I need to figure out what really happened yesterday. Seeing Keela's house, or the lawn where her boyfriend nearly killed me, might spark a memory. If not, I'll at least get to see her. Hopefully. Then, she can explain yesterday to me while I try not to do anything stupid. If I can manage to make it through the day without proposing to her or flying into a murderous rage, it'll be a success.

I start my engine and drive past the library, following the sidewalk Keela took as she strolled away from campus. I was so focused on how I knew her and what I might say to her that I wasn't paying attention to my surroundings. I remember every move her body made, though. The cracks in the concrete that her feet avoided. The way her profile looked when she made this left-hand turn. If Keela was my GPS, I'd definitely never be lost. Unless forced to pay attention to traffic on the road around me instead of being allowed to stare at the sidewalk. I should have made the trip on foot but I don't want to become the ball of sweat I ended up being yesterday. My stench this morning was repulsive.

I make another turn and hope it's the right one. When I first saw her yesterday, I got that itchy burning sensation in my hand. If that was all real and not a byproduct of my head getting scrambled, the phenomenon was most definitely connected to Keela. I don't feel it today, though. If it comes back, that could mean I'm close. Right now, nothing around me looks familiar. I U-turn and head back the way I came, trying not to crash while doing my best to remember which street I followed Keela down yesterday. A raven swoops in front of my windshield and banks off to the right, flying low over the asphalt of the road at the next intersection. At this point, I have nothing to lose. Either Merrymont University has a bird problem or this raven is my guardian angel. Its flight path drew my attention to Keela yesterday and we'll see if it takes me to her again today. Crazier things have happened. I think.

I hit my blinker and make a quick right, speeding after the raven. It gives its wings a hard flap and shoots off to the left. I make the same turn and watch the sky. The raven dips behind a row of trees and disappears. I take a deep breath. Following the bird was a gamble and so far, it isn't paying off. I grab my phone. Despite being plugged in, it isn't charging. This old truck doesn't have a navigation system, so without my phone I can't even pull over and review a map of these residential areas.

I stay on the street I'm on and follow it through the next intersection. The sidewalk tapers and the houses get larger. Just like yesterday. A jolt of excitement rushes through me. I scan the houses and smile in relief when the big white house comes into view. I'm going to have to grab a bag of birdseed for my new pet raven. I park on the street in front of Keela's house. In my quest to unravel fact from fiction, I can now confirm that Keela's house is as real as she is. The place looks exactly the same as I remember. Three stories high. White siding. Stone walkway. Red brick columns holding up the porch roof, and two massive wooden doors beyond the columns.

I open my door and get out of the truck, scanning the yard as I walk up the stone path leading to the front porch. In the spot where I thought I encountered Aether, there are no scorch marks on the grass. That could mean I didn't see him here, or it could mean he was here but not because he stepped out of a sizzling oval of light.

I walk up the steps and pause in front of the doors. I don't relish the idea of interacting with Keela's brothers again, but I also don't want to stand out here waiting for her like some kind of creep. If I'd just approached her at Merrymont yesterday, I wouldn't be out here trying to sort through which of my memories are real. I lift my fist and knock. I'm not going to stand here debating my thoughts. That's what got me in trouble yesterday, too much thinking and not enough action.

No one answers the door. I knock again and wait, shifting my posture and rubbing my jaw as I look around. I didn't bother shaving again this morning. I'm already hoping for a lot of things today, but I can add hoping Keela likes a five o'clock shadow to the list. I knock for the third time and then shove my hands into my pockets to keep from fidgeting. I don't see any cameras but the hair on the back of my neck is standing on end, telling me that I'm being watched. If it's Keela, I want to seem confident. Not like there's a nest of ants in my pants. I'm typically not a nervous guy but all things considered, I'm on edge.

Time drags on. The door isn't opening of its own accord this time and no one is answering it either. A sickening feeling crawls through my stomach. *What if they're all in the cave again?* I shake the thought loose. Even if this house was built around the mouth of a cave, everything else about yesterday's experience inside of it can't be real.

I turn my back to the door and look around the neighborhood. I guess it's possible for a cave system to be running underneath all of these homes. I'd ask someone but the whole place is as quiet today as it was yesterday. *Odd.* You'd think there would at least be a gardener tending to one of the gardens but there isn't. I don't see one single person or any sign of life at all for that matter. It's way too silent here.

I face the door again and tug one hand from my pocket, knocking, and leaning close to the door to see if I can hear anyone inside. I can't. The wood is too thick. Against my better judgment, I try the handles. Both doors are locked. *Good.* Even if the door would have popped open like it did yesterday, I'd already promised myself that I wouldn't go inside again. A promise my growing frustration would have just broken had either door been unlocked.

I don't want to be rude and keep knocking, and it's obvious no one is going to answer the door, but someone has to be here. I lift my fist and bang out one final knock. As expected, no one answers. I turn and jog back down the steps, watching the eerily quiet neighborhood as I traipse back to my truck. Something is very wrong here. There are no vehicles in any of the driveways, toys spread over lawns, or muffled sounds of music playing while someone cleans their house. I get to my truck and slide behind the wheel. My eyes scan the windows of Keela's house, looking for any sign of movement. There is none. The place seems abandoned. The same as the rest of the neighborhood.

I drop my gaze to the pine trees concealing most of the structure. They're thick and full, like an impenetrable army of limbs and trunks protecting what now seems more like a fortress than a home. I have the distinct impression that if someone entered that green army's territory, they'd never find their way back out again.

I start the truck and redo the plug on my phone. It still won't charge. I'm going to have to go get a new one, and I need to do that now so I can grab some food before heading to orientation. I glance back at the house. I'd like to wait, but I worked too hard to get into Merrymont not to attend my first required meeting. I could write my number on a piece of paper and leave it here, asking Keela to call me. Her brothers might intercept the note, though. If I leave it for her, I'll also spend all of my waking hours staring at my phone, terrified I'll miss her call. Whatever spell she put me under yesterday, it's threatening to wreck my whole world. The best thing I can do for myself is leave here, get a phone, and go to orientation. Because if Keela does show up, I'm liable to throw away my future in favor of staying right here with her. That's a scary truth to admit. One I need to keep at the forefront of my mind. Maybe I should heed Leah's warning. Keela is trouble. I haven't even talked to her yet and already I'm making terrible life choices.

I shift into gear and drive away, forcing myself not to look back. Keela is a part of my future, I know she is. I'm just not certain that future needs to happen right now. Maybe it needs to wait until after graduation. She has a boyfriend anyway. Maybe in four years, their relationship will have run its course and I won't have to kill him to get him away from her.

O rientation is about as boring as I expected it to be. Even the parts when the campus police chief impersonated a drunk college student attempting to lie about being drunk. He drew laughter from the other students but none of this has been amusing for me, let alone informative. I'm here, though, and thankfully it's nearly over.

I finish setting up my new phone and send Collin a text to ask when he's going to be back. Him distracting me is the only chance I have of staying away from Keela because even as I sit here telling myself to focus on the sound of the dean's voice, if not her words, all I'm managing to do is make myself sick with thoughts of never setting eyes on Keela's face again. The fear is real, and it's threatening to ruin my college career more than Leah and thumbtacks ever could. Every thought I have either begins or ends with Keela. It's unnerving but yet I welcome it. By the time Collin gets back he's going to have to chain me up in the basement of Sigma Beta Λύκος.

Right after Collin first came to Merrymont, I visited and found myself wandering around the big old fraternity house. There was a large empty room in the basement with chains bolted into the floor and walls, shackles dangling open on the ends of those chains. He said it was part of the hazing. They take new recruits down there and pretend they're going to lock them up. In my case, if the shackles work, Collin may need to restrain me for real.

I set my phone on my knee and scrub my jaw. When the lady at the kiosk took the back off of my old phone, she made a face and told me the thing looked like I'd stuck it in a microwave. My first thought was that Keela's phone might be damaged too, and that even if it wasn't, she still might like a new one. When I stopped to put gas in the truck, my first thought was of whether or not Keela has a vehicle and if her tank needed topped off. My mom always hated stopping for fuel so Dad kept her tank filled, a job I took on after he died. I guess it's in my blood to want to take care of my partner and I don't mind being lovesick for the right person, but despite how I feel, Keela has a say in whether or not she's mine and I've never even had a conversation with her, so I really shouldn't be at this level of devotion.

I stretch out the fingers of my left hand, inspecting the top of it where I'd been itching and burning yesterday. I haven't felt so much as a tingle from that spot today. "Dude," a voice rattles close to my ear. My knee jerks and my phone tumbles to the carpeted floor of the auditorium. I spin in my seat. Gelby smiles from where his arms are folded over the back of the seat next to mine. "Those fat little stubs on the end of your hand are fingers. In case this meeting is so boring your mind is too numb to remember."

I lean over and pinch him. Hard. "Ouch," he whines. "What was that for?"

I pinch my own arm equally hard. It hurts. Not hallucinating then. Right? "Nothing," I mumble. "Just checking."

He rubs the red spot on his arm. "Checking for what? How many times you can pinch a friend before getting punched in the face?"

I reach for my phone. "I met you once and from what I remember, it wasn't a pleasant experience, so we're hardly friends."

He takes out his phone and types into it. Mine vibrates with a notification. *You wound me, Sean.*

I glare at him. "Is this message from you?"

My phone vibrates again. *Yes. Save my number, friend.* I shake my head at him, holding my tongue as orientation ends and students begin to noisily file out of the auditorium.

Once it's quiet enough not to be yelling at him, I lift out of my seat, keeping an eye on him. "What are you doing here?"

He looks around as if he's confused. "Attending orientation. Isn't that what all the freshmen are doing today?"

I sit back down. "You're a student here? A freshman?"

One of his golden eyebrows slowly begins to rise. "Are you okay? Did you hit your head or something?"

I shove out of my seat and spin toward the walkway, colliding with a hulking frame whose body heat is about as hot as I feel right now. *Haldir.* I scan his nostrils. "Let me guess, you just happen to be a freshman, too?"

He doesn't answer and there's no smoke boiling out of his nose so I turn back to Gelby. "What's the secret to getting your brother to walk and talk like a real boy? Because I didn't hit my head hard enough to stand here taking any crap from either of you."

Gelby's eyes shift briefly to Haldir before coming back to mine, the hard edge to them falling away and becoming friendly again. "Dude, why are you so hostile today? Hal and I came to see if you want to go hang with us at Skald's Bar. You know, throw back a few beers and blow off some steam. Especially after sitting through this." He flicks his hand toward the stage at the front of the room. "It was all I could do not to heckle them the whole time. Hal could have put on a better presentation." Gelby's eyes glitter with amusement when he looks at his brother. "The ladies certainly would have preferred him to be the one standing up there. He tends to draw them in without ever opening his mouth. It's a gift, really. Mind telling us how you do that, Hal?"

His brother grunts and Gelby chuckles. "What do you say, Sean? Will you hang out with us tonight? My brother Rohan is meeting us at Skald's and Hal here is in a mood because he likes to get there while the girls are still hot and the beer is still cold."

I want to say no. Based on what Collin said about them, I *should* say no. But these are Keela's brothers so despite how this feels like a setup, I'm going. I stuff my phone into my back pocket. "I've heard about Skald's from my friend Collin. He says it's pretty cool and I've wanted to check it out, but I need to run back to my dorm first. I'll meet you guys over at the bar in half an hour."

I watch Gelby for any sign that he's not on board with me walking to the bar on my own, but he only smiles. "Sounds great. Tell Collin to come by, too. The more, the merrier."

Haldir steps away from me. I move past him and out into the aisle. I want to know if Keela is going to be at Skald's but it's probably a bad idea to ask them about her. I'll just have to go find out on my own. "I'll let Collin know where we'll be, and I'll see you in thirty minutes."

Although I'm still only in a t-shirt, it's a fresh, clean one. Acceptable attire for a place like Skald's. Though the bar scene has never been my thing, this is college. I figured at some point during my time at Merrymont I'd find myself visiting all the local watering holes, and Collin told me this one is more tolerable than the others around here. Back when I was able to get ahold of him. I called once I got to my dorm but he still hasn't responded to me. Sometimes we go more than a week without speaking but it's rare for us not to answer each other when either of us reaches out.

I walk toward the sound of the music, surprised to see a line already forming outside of the bar. Despite the fact that Collin can hold his alcohol better than anyone else I know, he tends to prefer small, private parties over the ruckus of a crowded bar. For him to frequent Skald's, I made an assumption about the place and expected it to be a much more low-key kind of affair. Instead, I could hear the music from a block away and the line of people waiting to get inside is wrapped halfway around the side of the building. It's barely happy hour. I see now why Haldir wanted to get here so early.

I cut toward the back of the line but stop when I hear a girl with dark brown hair excitedly exclaiming to her friend. "Haldir just looked at me! Should I go talk to him?" I follow her line of sight and spot Hal leaning against the building next to Gelby. They're up by the front door and they're both watching me. Gelby spreads a smile across his lips but Haldir doesn't attempt to hide the fact that they were both quite happy to stand there studying me instead of calling out like a normal friend would do if they were waiting for you. Game on because they aren't the only curious ones. I want to figure out who these two are and why they sought me out today. They do look my age but I'm not buying the story that they both happen to be freshmen. The unrealistic side of me wants to believe that Keela mentioned having a crush on me so her brothers are vetting me for her. I doubt that's the case but a guy can hope. Especially when all of his roads lead to Keela.

I approach the two men. Haldir's arms are crossed and he moves his eyes from me to scan the crowd behind me, looking more like a sentinel than someone out to have a good time. Beside him, Gelby shoves off the wall. "Aw, did you change your shirt and put on cologne just for us?"

I flick a hand to the girls standing in line. "All I can say is I'm glad I didn't do it for them. They only have eyes for Haldir and I can't compete with that." Maybe flattering him will loosen him up a little.

Gelby motions to the door. "Let's go inside. Maybe our luck with the ladies will be better in here."

I reach for my wallet but the doorman looks at Gelby, who nods. The man stands back and waves me through, his eyes diverting away from us as Haldir flanks me. I tuck my wallet away. "I assume you two are regulars here?"

Gelby looks over his shoulder with what I'm learning is his trademark grin. "Regular might not be quite the right word."

We cross through a foyer area that has two leather sofas on either side of it with a sign above each indicating the seating is for those waiting for a designated driver. I'm impressed with the thoughtfulness and a little taken aback by the man who is already curled up on the leather to my right. He must have started drinking early. We pass through a set of double doors and enter a large room ringed with tables and booths. To our left is a bar that runs the length of that side of the building, curving around the back wall for about five feet where there's a hallway that leads deeper into the building. There are two very burly guards positioned at the mouth of that hallway and directly behind them is a set of stairs. That must be how you get up to the VIP area overlooking this main floor, and that must be why Collin likes Skald's. I'd bet my entire savings account on the fact that he comes in, gets cleared for the VIP room, and never comes back down into the fray.

Gelby catches me scanning the tinted windows of the floor above us. "Is that how you normally party? Tucked away all by yourself in the exclusive section?"

I shake my head and scan the rest of the bar, the sight of the pool tables on the opposite side of the building bringing back a memory of Keela wielding a pool stick as if it were a spear. I'm not sure why I'd imagine something like that. I mean, she was hot throwing the stick, but she'd also be hot in a hallucination where she was crawling onto my lap. I clear my throat and pray that imagery leaves me before I mess up and tell her brothers just how hot their sister is. "I um...don't really party enough to have any usuals, but it seems like you guys come here a lot. Are you the VIP sort?"

Haldir makes a groaning sound and moves off toward the bar. Gelby chuckles. "The answer to that question would depend on your perspective."

I raise a brow at him. "What does that mean? Do you guys own the bar or something?"

He shrugs. "Something. Important people do prefer to be upstairs though. Or rich ones. Your buddy Collin MacKenzie usually hangs out up there."

Unease curls through my gut. Something in the way he said Collin's name doesn't sit right with me. "I'm not surprised. Collin has been my best friend since were eight, so I can attest to the fact that he has particular tastes. He's also an acquired taste. So it's cool if you don't like him, but to me, he's a brother. I won't tolerate his name getting dragged in front of me."

Gelby holds up his hands. "No dragging. I'm just here to have a good time while getting to know my new buddy. See how well it's working so far? I already know you're loyal to a big-headed punk. Hard to say what else I'll find out about you by the end of the night."

I glare at him and he laughs, motioning to the bar where Haldir is pouring his own shots from a bottle of liquor that he might as well be drinking from. He throws back a shot, slams the glass onto the bar top, refills it, and repeats his process two more times before Gelby draws my attention away from the scene Haldir is making. "What's your poison? And I'm not talking about the alcohol. What kind of women do you like?"

Your sister. I don't dare say my thoughts out loud. Instead, I move into the empty space Haldir has commanded around him. He isn't friendly so I'm not surprised that even the women who find him attractive are moving off and giving him a wide berth. I am a little surprised that the men are also giving up their ground so easily. It's crowded in here and there isn't much space at the bar as it is. "I don't have a type. I have instinct. I know what I like when I see it."

Gelby walks to Haldir's right and reaches over the heads of a group of ladies seated at the bar, gesturing to the bartender for two beers. "And have you seen anything you like tonight?"

"Leah," I sputter when she whips around on her stool. Since I saw her last, she's cut her hair. It now hangs at an angle and only an inch above her shoulders.

Gelby yanks his arm back, his elbow clipping the top of her head. "Well, if it isn't Leah MacKenzie. Is she why you're so close to her brother? And does he know his sister is such a little...fox?"

Anger burns in Leah's eyes. Gelby clipped her good and normally I'd be all for making him apologize, but Leah is the last person who needs a guy defending her. She can handle Gelby on her own because the females in Collin's family have always been more aggressive than the males, and the ones more apt to cause a fight than not. They're vocal and ruthless, willing to do anything to get the upper hand. I don't care to see Leah get into a down-and-dirty fight tonight, though, because if she does, I'll have to answer to Collin for not stopping her. He'll guess that she started yet still expect me to keep her from it. In this case, Gelby technically started it. I step between him and her. "Cool it, Leah. He didn't mean to bump you and I'm really not in the mood to have to listen to your mouth again, so just turn back around and keep having fun with your friends."

She slides off her stool, teeth clenched and her words nothing more than a hiss as she pulls herself up to glare directly into my eyes. "What are you doing with him?"

Gelby snakes his arm around my shoulders. "Funny you should ask. I was just talking to my buddy Sean here about the type of women he likes, and then poof, here you are. What a coincidence!"

She growls at him. He removes his arm and holds up his hands. "Don't shoot the wingman. I'm just trying to help out my boy."

Annoyance streams into my already tense muscles. I am *not* attracted to Leah and it's time to set that record straight. For him, her, and everyone else. I open my mouth, shutting it again when her face falls, doubt and fear chasing each other across her features. I've never seen Leah be vulnerable and now I feel bad for being the cause of whatever is going on inside her head. I rest a hand on her shoulder. "Leah, I..." A shiver races through her. I wouldn't have caught it if I wasn't touching her, but I can still feel her trembling under my touch. I know she isn't afraid of me any more than she's secretly harboring feelings for me. So what has the self-possessed Leah MacKenzie shaken?

I follow her gaze over my shoulder, angling away from her to see whatever it is she's looking at. Behind me, there's a figure cloaked in a dark hood. I can see nothing inside the shadows the wide hood is casting over her face, but even without Rohan's presence at her side, I would know this figure anywhere. "Keela," I whisper her name, finding myself just as shaken as Leah.

Rohan scans my arm. All the way up to where my palm is still resting on Leah's shoulder. I rip it away and decide I'm not going to let his glowering stop me. Keela is standing here in front of me and I'm finally getting my chance to speak to her. "Hey... I mean, hi. Um, hello." *Smooth, Sean. Real smooth.*

I try again but Leah's nails dig into my arm just above my elbow, her words still coming out between clenched teeth. "Sean, can I talk to you?" She steps closer to my side and slightly in front of me, facing Keela as she adds, "In private."

Keela moves toward us, the fabric of her deep green cargo pants as silent as the night. If Leah's body wasn't pressed against mine, I'm not sure she'd be able to stay on her feet as Keela eats up our personal space. Her black boots stop directly in front of me and I can't help but scan the length of her body. The tall boots wrap up her legs and lace just beneath her knees, the pants continuing from there until they disappear under the hem of her hooded jacket. Every inch of Keela is covered except for her hands, and yet she's the most attractive woman in the room. She reaches up and flips the hood off her head. My heart skips a dozen beats. She smiles and it skips a dozen more. Even when Keela's smile is fake, it's enough to make me want to drop to my knees. What's better is hearing her melodic voice. "Is that a new hairstyle, Leah? It looks so similar to mine, and yet I'm sure that the last time I saw you coming back from a *private* rendezvous, your hair was a little longer." She tilts her head. "Wasn't it, Gelby?"

He steps around me and runs his fingers through Leah's hair. "It was."

As much as I don't want to look away from Keela, I have to. I'm not a fan of Leah's and she can normally take care of herself, but she isn't herself tonight. Even if what's happening to her is a dose of much-deserved karma, she's still my best friend's sister. Her being taunted by another female is much different than Gelby getting in on the action. "Don't touch her."

Leah tugs at my arm, her nails sinking deeper into my skin. "Let's go."

I yank her claws out of me. "No. Everyone just needs to settle down."

She spits a curse at me and circles behind my back, storming off with a well-placed elbow into Gelby's side. He rubs at the spot. "I guess your girlfriend is sensitive about her hair. Do you need to go after her? I'll hold your beer for you while you go smooth things over."

I narrow my eyes at him. "She's not my girlfriend, and you know that already." I face Keela, my hand automatically reaching for her. Haldir comes out of nowhere and slams into me, throwing me into the stool Leah had been sitting on earlier. I spring upright and go at him. "What is your problem?"

Gelby slams a hand against each of our advancing chests. "Not here."

"Fine," I bite. "Let's go outside, *Hal*, because it's time someone taught you some manners."

Gelby laughs, and he isn't the only one. I look over at Rohan and catch the amusement painted on his face. Then I look at Keela and catch the slight roll of her eyes just before Haldir jabs a meaty finger in my face. "Never touch her."

I swat his finger away, speaking to Keela from behind her two brothers. If this is the only shot I have at her, so be it. She's the one who walked up to me and I don't know what's going on between Leah and her, but I do know I don't want Keela walking away from this with the wrong impression. "Leah is my best friend's sister," I explain. "That's all. I'm not involved with her and I have no desire to be."

Rohan is no longer amused. He's asserting himself and answering for his sister. "Keela doesn't care."

She sighs. "Keela is right here and can answer for herself." Her eyes meet mine. "He's right, I don't care who you date." She says the words but for the briefest of moments, I see her pupils dilate. Her mouth opens ever so slightly and I'm certain she feels something for me. I hope it's the same thing I'm feeling for her. I want to ask but she flips the hood back over her head and spins away from me, disappearing into the crowd of people behind us.

I meet the dark depths of Haldir's eyes. "Happy now? Instead of being here safe with us, she's ticked off and out there with all of *them* because her idiot brother is drunk and acting like a moron. And that's me telling you what I think of you in the nicest way I can put it."

Rohan skulks away with a groan and Gelby gives Haldir and me both a shove. "I'm not going to bother with niceties. You're both imbeciles. As entertaining as that is, I need to go see a lady about a thing. You two have some drinks and try not to kill each other while I'm gone." He pats Haldir's shoulder. "There are too many witnesses here, so go easy on the kid."

"Kid?" I rip, but Gelby trots off and leaves me facing only Haldir. His hard stare doesn't leave mine for two more long and suffocating breaths. With a final narrowing of his eyes, he turns away from me and looks out over the bar. I find myself stepping in line with him, the two of us scanning the crowd in the direction Keela went. I can't find her. Maybe he can. "Someone out there is definitely going to touch her."

Haldir's chest rumbles. "No. She will touch them, and if I'm not drunk, I will kill them."

He stalks back to his spot at the bar and I watch as he tosses back more liquor as if it's nothing stronger than water. Not even Collin could drain a bottle the way Haldir is and remain on his feet, but Haldir's drinking is none of my concern. He has brothers here. They should be the ones monitoring him because Gelby isn't the only one who needs to see a lady about a thing.

I turn away from Haldir and scan the bar once again. There's a crowd near the pool tables in the back but I don't think that's where Keela went. My attention draws up to the tinted windows of the VIP section. She didn't get up there via the stairs behind the bar. I would have seen her. Still, I can't help but trust my instincts. My gut says Keela is up there. I glance at Haldir. He puts the bottle to his lips and turns it up, draining it. I want to leave him here, but I need him. "Can you get us upstairs?"

He turns and rests his elbows on the bar, still looking lucid despite the drained bottle of Jack in his meaty grip. His eyes focus on the tinted windows above us as if he can see through them. "Yes."

I nudge him. "Well, then?"

He sighs. "If I have to endure this place and babysit you, I might as well do it comfortably. Let's go."

He pushes off the bar and we approach the curved end where the two guards are stationed. They each give Haldir a nod right before a screech stops us both. It's a high-pitched sound that only a girl can make, and from the way she's shouting Haldir's name, she sounds like one I don't want to be anywhere near. Haldir's dark scowl says he doesn't either. "Hi," the breathless girl with hair the same color of sand as mine says against his shoulder. "Irene called and I didn't believe her when she said you were here tonight. I've been trying to reach you but no one has your number and—"

"That's because I don't want to be reached," he cuts her off. "Go home, Daphne. This is no place for you or Irene."

I glance over Daphne's shoulder and spot two women who are smiling brightly in our direction. The blonde flips her hair over her shoulder but both women seem a bit shy about approaching us. I understand how they feel. It's always awkward approaching a stranger, and that's why guys will hang on to any thread of attention from a girl, using it to work up their nerve. A passing glance. A polite smile. Even if a girl is putting off a very clear *stay away* vibe, our man brains will convince us she's not directing that vibe at us. I might very well be doing that with Keela, and the fact that I'm prepared to justify my actions toward her is a pretty clear indicator that I am, but I assume one of the two girls smiling at me right now is Irene and I have no interest in sticking around here for introductions. There's one person I want to speak to and my heart says she's upstairs.

Before I get roped into the largely one-sided conversation the clueless Daphne is trying to have with Haldir, I take a chance on passing by the guards alone. They each stare holes through me but they don't stop me from climbing the carpeted stairs. My shoulders relax. Them seeing me approach with Haldir was enough, and now all I have to do is make it to the top of the stairs to find out whether or not my instincts are right.

12

Keela

I stalk through the bar. Even without Rohan's presence behind me, most in this crowd would still be leery of me. Moreso if I show my face and confirm for them that is indeed me cloaked within this hood. Revealing myself would draw the males to me. Then their females would grow enraged, though none of them would be willing to engage me any more than Leah MacKenzie did tonight. The shifters are predators and they don't normally fear a lone Vampir, but I am unique. Some of the stories told of me are true, others exaggerated, but none of them are devoid of the fact that I am an apex predator, unlike anything most races have ever known because Vampir keep to themselves, living in nests mostly outside of Midgard.

I pass through the bar and shove out the emergency exit into the alleyway. Only the oldest of my kind can walk in the sunlight, something I didn't know I could do until Bishop rescued me from the Isle of Misery. I lived there in total darkness and on the constant brink of starvation. For how long, I do not know. Nothing marked the passing of my time and when other exiles came to the Isle, I stayed hidden away until the hunger drove me to them. Those who survived called me Dauði. *Death*. It was Rohan who named me Keela. He said it meant beautiful. I thought nothing of it until Haldir, my confidant, professed his love. Next came Rohan himself, Alberich, and so many of the creatures under Bishop's rule. Vampir should not be able to enthrall any species but humans, and yet here I am, unable to shut it off. Not even Gelby's magic can mask me. He's spent years teaching me to wield magic on my own, and I can only hope that I'll be able to one day have a real relationship with someone. One based on actually being liked for who and what I am, not one that's simply a product of my allure.

I don't speak to Rohan as I press my hand to the wall beside our secret door. The blue siding of Skald's Bar shimmers and we both walk through the exterior wall to the set of stairs that lead to the VIP room. "Keela," Rohan says my name softly as we ascend. "You need to feed. If you want no one from the bar, allow me to feed you."

"No."

"Please," he begs.

"No." I press my hand to the wall of the VIP room and when it shimmers, I waste no time moving inside. We asked that it be left empty for us tonight, so I don't bother looking around. No one would go against the wishes of the Vasilis.

Rohan places his hand on my arm. "I am always here for you."

I pull away from him and move to the tinted window overlooking the bar. All of my brothers have fed me in the past but I now only allow Gelby, and only when I have no other choice. I require more blood than most Vampir, and Álfr blood is strong. Vasilis blood, especially so. But feeding is intimate for me, and oftentimes more so for those I'm drawing blood from. My mouth on their skin arouses them and when I pierce their flesh, my venom is ecstasy. Even those I intend to drain end up begging me not to stop. It takes all of my concentration not to be sucked into my own desires. The men I feed from don't want me, they want the lie that is me. On the occasions when I give in and allow myself to choose someone I want to spend a torrid night with, I always heal their punctures and compel them to forget they ever met me.

"I will choose someone," I tell Rohan. With a heavy sigh, he plods across the room and sits in a booth. I don't have to look to know that he's where he has the best Keela-viewing vantage point. All of my brothers say the affection they have for me is real. For the most part, it is. But Gelby is the only one not drawn to me as Rohan and Haldir are. I rarely encounter a male of any kind who isn't enthralled with me and when I do, they never have a drop of romantic interest. I've asked Gelby if I repulse him and he says all I do is annoy him as any little sister would. Which never fails to make me laugh because from what I've researched about my kind, I may be older than all of the boys Bishop brought me to live with.

I'm certainly older than Sean Winkle, and yet I can't stop thinking about the human. He smells of wolf and his room reeks of Leah MacKenzie. The Ulfr has marked him as her territory but underneath her heady scent, I smell his. I didn't open my senses to him until he followed me into the woods. Once his scent hit my nose, my mouth watered and my fangs extended. If Aether hadn't been waiting for me, I probably would have dragged the human into the forest and had my way with him. A dangerous position for both of us. I haven't been consumed by bloodlust in a very long time but something in Sean Winkle triggered me. It was all I could do to keep from sinking my teeth into Aether. He wouldn't have minded, I've had my fair share of fun feeding from him. Hiding from my brothers is draining, though, and I wasn't prepared for it the day I met the human. My only option was to attack Aether's mouth with my own and wait for my brothers to show up. I knew my anger at their meddling would override the lust, and the human would be safe from the monster I am.

I close my eyes and open my senses to the bar. Gelby's essence is easy enough to pick out and remove. He's enjoying the wolf. The taunting. The teasing. He took her to the gray house last night instead of returning to our home, but I could smell Leah MacKenzie on him. Her scent. Their sex. Gelby's arousal when he toyed with her again tonight. He isn't yet finished playing with the Ulfr. If her kind held anything other than contempt for me, I'd feel sorry for her. I know too well what it is to be nothing more than a trinket. Gelby will not force Leah to do anything she doesn't want to do, though, and with the way she's spreading her scent all over Sean Winkle and everything he owns, it's abundantly clear to me that Leah likes to play games. She's coated the boy so every other Ulfr female knows he belongs to her, as well as many other races we live with in harmony here in Midgard. Yet Leah isn't with Sean Winkle tonight. She's with Gelby, putting her hands all over him so others will see her with a Vasilis. My brothers rarely interact publicly and no doubt, Rohan will speak to Gelby about this later, but their drama does not concern me. I continue to search through the stench of sweat and arousal, eliminating Haldir and many others as my thirst searches for the blood that will quench it tonight. This is much easier when Alberich has prisoners I can feed from. Sometimes he even allows me to drain their bodies of blood before he feasts on those who have been sentenced to death for their crimes against Midgard.

My pulse begins to rise and my fangs extend. I open my eyes. Sean Winkle looks as delicious as he smells. Which is precisely why I shouldn't make eye contact with him again. If I could compel him to forget me, maybe I'd succumb to my lust. For some reason my compulsion doesn't work on him and even if it did, there would still be the possibility of me accidentally killing him. The Vasilis are to protect humans, not murder them in the height of passion. Still, Sean is heading this way and heat is blooming in my breast. "Human incoming," I warn Rohan. We're all supposed to be here doing recon on the boy while also gathering any intel we can about last night's Draugr attack. So far, none of us are doing much of anything. I'll be virtually useless until I feed. The hunger grows worse as the boy nears. I can smell the blood pumping through his veins and I want nothing more than to spill it across my lips while my tongue laps it from his neck.

I shut down my senses. I may not be able to control the thrall I have over this boy or any other, but I can control my own lust. I *will* control it.

Sean

Haldir isn't putting out anything that should encourage a woman, yet Daphne is still trying to get her hooks into him. More than that, and despite the fact that he isn't being nice to her, he's still standing beside her. Maybe he likes her after all. I hope so. That might keep him away from the VIP area, and I could really use that right now because my gut was right. Keela is here.

I cross the landing at the top of the stairs and sweep my gaze around the room. There are a handful of circular booths tucked along the back wall. Each is enclosed by its own partition and well spaced from the next. In the dim lighting of the booth closest to me, I see blue velvet upholstery and a dark wood table. The music from downstairs is just loud enough to cover any private conversations had inside this room, and it's clear that privacy is the very point of this section of Skald's. I can imagine Collin tucked into one of the booths with a woman under each arm. Unlike me, he prefers to have constant companionship, and fairly often those companions are of the female variety.

I walk toward Keela, allowing myself to take all of her in. She's standing by the windows exactly where I thought she would be. Her black jacket is unzipped and her hood is falling softly around her shoulders rather than covering her beautiful head. Underneath the jacket is a strappy tank top that looks similar to the sexy one she had on the last time I saw her. She doesn't acknowledge my approach and I already know her brothers won't like me walking up to her, but I've spent a lifetime dealing with the MacKenzie family, so I don't care how wealthy her family is or how big Haldir's biceps are. The only way I'll stop pursuing her is if she tells me to herself. In very clear words so I don't get confused and convince myself that what she really wants is for me to chase her with more conviction than anyone else ever has.

I step into place beside her. "Hi."

She keeps her eyes on the windows in front of us. "You've already said hello to me, Sean Winkle. In three different ways. I think that will suffice."

A noise comes from one of the booths and I glance that way. Rohan is relaxed against the velvet of the booth directly behind us, his arms stretched wide over the back of the seat and his icy eyes fixed on mine. The corner of his mouth is turned up and I don't have to guess why. He's enjoying his sister's cool indifference to me. We'll see how he feels when her hand is in mine and I'm leading her out of this place to somewhere that's actually private.

I reposition, giving him my back so he knows I intend to completely ignore him. I came here for a purpose and I intend to fulfill the mission. "You're right, Keela. I tripped over my tongue when I saw you tonight. If you don't hold that against me, I promise I'll figure out how to put one word in front of the other. Before you know it, we'll be having a full-blown conversation."

"Why?"

Her question throws me off. "Why should you not hold my bumbling against me? Or why do I want to talk to you?"

She lifts one delicate shoulder and her jacket slips off of it. My mouth waters with desire at the sight of her skin, but the woman herself is making no more of a move to answer my question than she is to fix the jacket. That's fine. I'm happy to take care of both for her. I run my fingers along the fabric of her sleeve and lift the jacket back over her shoulder, wanting more than anything to be doing the opposite. I want to undress her and admire every inch of her. In a private spot where her stupid brothers aren't milling around watching every move I make. "I want to talk to you because talking to you feels right. *We* feel right. I want to figure out why that is." My voice comes out huskier than I intend. "I want to know you, Keela."

Her eyes snap to mine. In the next second her hand slams into my chest and I fly backward across the room. My head collides with the wall and I shout, not for my own pain but for Keela. I don't know what I did wrong or how in the hell she's so strong. "Keela, I..." My apology fades on my lips. It's too late. She's gone.

Rohan and Haldir are standing in the middle of the room, their arms crossed. "No. Touching," they say in unison.

I rub the back of my head. "Yeah, I think I finally understand that."

"No *anything*," Haldir growls.

I meet his glare. I get that Keela is his sister, but he's acting like a jealous lover instead of a brother. "Keela is eighteen, right?"

"Age doesn't give you the right to lay hands on her," Rohan answers.

"Or any other part of your puny human body," Haldir adds.

My biceps flex of their own accord. "I'm hardly puny, and I wasn't putting any part of my body on your *sister*. I was attempting to have a conversation with her and, apparently, I said something that upset her so excuse me while I go find her and apologize because so long as she's eighteen, she can make her own damn decisions about who talks to her and who puts what on her body."

13

Keela shoved me in the direction of the stairwell and I didn't see her go past me, but she must have because there's no other way out of the VIP room. I trudge down the stairs, determined not to let Rohan or Haldir stop me. My ego is both bolstered and bruised. I spoke to Keela and she spoke back. It wasn't a great start but it was happening, and it would have gone better had I reigned myself in. Now she's upset and I have a knot on my head. At this rate, I'll start hallucinating again soon and see Santa Claus land his sleigh in the middle of the bar.

Gelby approaches me. "Who are you looking for?"

"Your sister," I snap. "Spare me your opinion on that fact. I've heard enough from your brothers and I don't care what any of you think. Keela is upset with me and I need to find her." Leah catches my eye. She's standing nearby and cocking her head this way as if she can eavesdrop on us inside the noisy bar. "Keela wouldn't leave here alone, would she?"

Gelby glances up to the VIP section. "She might. What did you do to her?"

I scrub my hands through my hair and turn in a circle, looking for her. "I said something she wasn't ready to hear and now she's... It isn't safe for her to walk home alone. She knows that, right? She wouldn't just take off without telling one of you."

He lets out a soft laugh. "No, I'm sure the damsel is somewhere nearby, waiting for us to escort her home so she doesn't have to walk the dark streets alone."

Daphne walks over to Leah, hoisting her hands onto her hips. I shake my head at Gelby and open my mouth to tell him how much I don't appreciate his sarcastic tone, but a flash of darkness rolls across my vision and all I see is Keela. Excitement burns in her dilated eyes and she lifts a finger to my lips, the tip of her fingernail barely brushing against me. Her voice comes out in a purr and a wave of nausea washes over me. She sounds far away, like she's at the end of a tunnel and speaking to me over the clamor of rushing water. "You do not know me. You've never seen me before or heard my name, and should you ever see me again, I won't be familiar to you. I'm just another face in the crowd and you have no interest in me whatsoever."

My stomach rolls. I want to argue with her but all of this is too familiar. She's compelling me. Or trying to. My mouth flops open but no sound emerges. *Is this real?* I stare at her. Why would anyone believe they possess the power to make someone forget them? Sadness I don't understand crawls through her features. It's deep and so powerful it reaches inside me, destroying all hope of there ever being an *us*. Keela doesn't want me. I'm destined to love her, and she's destined to wreck me.

"Please," I beg, trying to force my mouth to form more words. She flips the hood of her jacket up, concealing her face in shadows. A pit opens in my chest. Air brushes against my cheeks and she's gone. Bar noise begins returning to my ears, louder than ever. A roar snaps my attention to the left. Leah slams a fist into Daphne's face and spins, crushing an elbow into one of Daphne's friends before charging the third. Gelby goes after her but she jumps on top of one of the pool tables, grabs the light fixture above her, and swings out until her feet come back around and connect with his face. Shouts erupt from all directions and an ogre of a man sends Leah's pool table crashing onto its side. Rohan and Haldir breeze by me and I just stand here, in the midst of growing pandemonium.

Someone bumps me from behind and I turn around, only to be slugged by a guy half my size. I palm his fist when he tries it again. "No, thanks. My head has been hit enough lately." I shove him away from me and weave through the brawlers who are destroying every piece of furniture in the bar. Leah's punch was like a bomb going off inside an arsenal. Despite still feeling like my stomach wants to relieve itself of everything I've had to eat this week, I go after her. She's more trouble than she's worth but I won't leave her in the middle of this war zone. I duck under the arm of a girl who is using her shoe to beat another girl in the face. Thankfully it's a floppy flat shoe and not a pointy stiletto. Rohan is up ahead, moving through the chaos, following after Haldir who is cutting a path through the crowd. For every man Haldir tosses aside, two more join in the fight. None of them touch the brothers, though, and from what I can tell, neither Haldir nor Rohan have any intention of getting into the middle of what quickly escalated into a bar-wide fight.

I fall in behind them. They're on a mission to get to Gelby and the last place I saw him was with Leah. I spot his ponytail, his hair standing out in the sea of heads before me. He's standing with his hands down at his sides, looking around him as if daring anyone to approach from any angle. No one is. The only fight-free zone in the bar exists within a four-foot radius of him. A scream rattles the rafters and I snap my head in the direction of Leah's voice. She brings an elbow down into some girl's face and then kicks her front leg forward, landing the heel of her booted foot at the base of some guy's sternum. Two girls jump her from behind, one of them grabbing a handful of Leah's now short hair and using it to slam Leah's face down into the wooden side of the toppled pool table. Blood splatters across the felt. I reach Leah at the same time Gelby does. People scatter and I cup Leah's face in my hands. Blood is pouring from her nose and down into her mouth, streaking her teeth with red as she smiles at me, her eyes wide and wild. I'm not surprised that she's enjoying this fight, but she'll regret it tomorrow when her broken nose is swollen and her body is sore.

I rip off my shirt and press it into her hands. "Use this to stop the bleeding." I swing her into my arms and cradle her head against my chest, blocking it from taking any more blows. "Hold on, I'm going to get you out of here."

She mutters something from beneath my shirt and I have no doubt it's an insult, but she doesn't try to claw out of my grip. She holds the t-shirt against her face and remains still as I rush us toward the exit. Gelby hasn't said a word but judging by the way the fighters are parting like the

Red Sea in front of me, I know he and his brothers are right behind me. Considering Leah slugged him, I'm not so sure that's a good thing.

We reach the foyer and I shove out the door and through the crowd of people still waiting to get inside. "You really don't want to go in there," I caution as I head for the opposite side of the road. It's hard to tell who's going to run out of the bar behind us or what state of amped they'll be. Plus, if I have to fight Gelby and his brothers to keep Leah from being hurt further, I'd rather do it over here where it'll be just us and not a whole parking lot of other people.

Leah slings her arms around my neck when I try to set her on her feet. I bend my knees and drop my arms from her. She hangs on for dear life, her legs scrabbling up my body and wrapping around my waist. "Knock it off," I warn. She was the catalyst for the whole scene inside the bar so the scared act isn't going to work on me. "I'm absolutely telling Collin about this and there's nothing you can do to stop that, so let go. I need to check your nose."

She drops her legs and slides down the front of me. Collin is younger but on the occasions when he gives Leah an order, usually one telling her to stop whatever it is she's doing, she listens to him. She'll buck the other siblings but not him.

I tug her arms from around my neck and lift her face. She sighs. "I'm fine. It's not broken."

"Pity," Gelby snarks from behind me.

I face him and his brothers. After everything that happened inside the bar, I'm not so sure it matters if I'm hallucinating about anything or not. There's no denying that there's something seriously off about this whole family. Including Keela. "Thanks for the help getting us out of the thick of that fight, but do any of you know where your sister is?"

Gelby's eyes sparkle and he runs them over Leah. "I always know where my sister is, and you seem to always know where this sister is. How sweet. The two of you are just adorable together. It must be unshakable love."

Frustration rattles through me and I swipe a hand down my face. Leah folds herself around me. "Ignore them. I want to go home. Please, Sean, will you take me home?"

I try to shake her loose. "All the way to Richlands home?"

She glances at Gelby and then up at me. "Yes, please. Let's go home."

I shift her to my side, hoping she'll let go of me, but she doesn't. She's anchored herself to me so tightly that a shot of doubt races through me. Maybe I'm wrong and Leah really is scared. She did have an uncharacteristic tremble earlier, but I've also never in my life had so much physical contact with her. Maybe she leads with aggression to hide the fact that she's actually a trembling mass of fear on the inside. "Fine." I give in. It isn't like I can leave her standing alone outside a bar. I give the three brothers a pointed look. "I'm not sure what happened tonight, but tell Keela I'm sorry."

None of them speak and I'm not surprised. If this compulsion thing is real, then I'm not even supposed to remember who Keela is. Compulsion isn't a real thing, though. I turn away from them and lead Leah down the sidewalk. "Did you drive here?"

Her hair tickles against my side as she shakes her head. "I walked from Sigma Beta Λύκος, but I don't want to go back there tonight."

I glance behind me. The brothers are gone. As much as I don't want to escort Leah anywhere, especially with her hugging me like this, I also don't want them following us. Gelby has some sort of an issue with the

MacKenzie family. I turn back around and pick up the pace. "Why did you hit Gelby?"

Leah nuzzles her way over my side and onto my bare chest, like a puppy rubbing itself against a leg. "He was in the way. I was being attacked by those girls and I didn't know if he was in on it or not."

I fight a wave of repulsion as she manages to push herself closer to my skin. "Why would Gelby be in on an attack against you? What did Daphne say to you?"

Her head springs away from my chest. "How do you know Daphne?"

I rest my arm against my chest, angling my elbow down between us to give myself a little breathing room. "She was talking to Haldir and he introduced us."

Leah's nails dig into my waist where she's glued herself to me. "Those girls are cats. Big dumb stupid cats who think men prefer them over me."

Her cold laugh sends a shiver through me. "Cats?"

She pushes away from me, her nails raking over my stomach as she does. "They're catty, Sean. You know the type."

That's true. I know way too many girls like Leah. I lead the way to my truck. "Hurry. Classes start tomorrow and at this rate, I won't make it back to campus until morning."

She hesitates. I turn to face her. "Not helping."

Her face falls. "Can I stay with you tonight?"

I gape at her. "No."

"Bu—"

"No," I cut her off. "What has gotten into you? And don't tell me you're scared because I'm not buying it."

She looks down at my bloody shirt crumpled in her fist. "I'm crashing at Collin's frat house while he's gone. That's where my car is. I can drive myself back to Richlands but I don't want to do it tonight, and I really don't want anyone in Sigma Beta Λύκος to see me like this." She looks up at me through her naturally thick lashes. "Let me stay here. Please? Just for tonight."

I study her. There are too many warring thoughts in my head right now. Part of me wants to put her in the truck and drive her home to her dad. Liam MacKenzie will put a stop to whatever is going on with his daughter. I doubt he even knows she's here because he wouldn't allow his prized firstborn daughter to stay in a frat house any more than he'd willingly let her spend a night with me. When Leah says Collin is the only member of her family who likes me, it's a true statement where Liam is concerned. He's never been outright mean to me, but he's never been friendly either. He regards me with what I can only describe as tolerant disdain. "If I let you stay here tonight, it's only for this one night."

Her eyes light up. "Okay."

I point at her. "If you lay so much as a finger on me, you're out. Do you understand?"

Her lips turn up. "No fingering you. Got it."

I search the internet for cases of humans claiming to be compelled by others. All sorts of things are coming up, but nothing describes what I've experienced with Keela. I wasn't coerced into doing anything for her, and

I feel no obligation to follow her orders. I don't feel constrained by the parameters of her words and I'm not obliged to forget her the way she seems to want me to.

"Those showers aren't half bad." Leah saunters into my room wearing one of my t-shirts and a pair of my gym shorts. The towel she's drying her hair with is my last clean one. I'm going to have to do laundry tomorrow and that's something I didn't plan on having to fit into my schedule on the very first day of classes. I look away from her and click off my laptop before she sees what I'm searching for.

She sits on my bed. "What were you doing with the Vasilis family tonight?"

I tuck my laptop away. "Who?"

She groans. "The people you came to Skald's with? They don't mingle with anyone, especially in public, so how is it that you got an invite to hang out with them?"

I shrug. "Maybe if you had my charming personality you'd get your own invitation."

She scoots back against the wall. "Gelby invited you, right? He's the only one of them with halfway decent manners."

I scan her nose. It looks remarkably normal. There's not even a bruise. "Why do you and Keela not get along?"

Her nostrils flare and her eyes narrow. "Isn't it obvious? She's a freak, and I don't hang out with losers."

I get up from the desk and bring my laptop with me. "Same. So do me a favor and be gone by the time I get back here in the morning."

Leah jumps off the bed. "Where are you going?"

I open the door. "You're up to something and I don't trust you, so I'm going to sleep in my truck."

She grabs the edge of the door, her free hand cupping the back of my last clean t-shirt. "Stay away from them, Sean. They're dangerous. Especially Keela."

14

I stare at the whiteboard hanging along the front wall of my astronomy class, my eyes unseeing after spending an uncomfortable night in my truck. I got very little sleep but at least Leah was gone when I finally went back to my room. She didn't make the bed this time, though, and I couldn't find the clothes I let her borrow last night. I won't be calling her to ask for them, either. As long as she stays out of my life, she can keep the clothes. I bought two new shirts from the library's gift shop this morning and they even had towels so I grabbed two more of those. Anything to put off doing laundry today. Leah's words of warning ping-ponged through my head all night and unfortunately for me, hers weren't the only words I kept replaying. I spent hours looking up accounts of compulsion and I even searched for the unfamiliar words Haldir and Rohan had used when I thought I walked into a fireplace and found them arguing with Keela. Not until this morning did I think to look up the symptoms of a head injury. It does appear to be possible for someone with a traumatic head wound to have vivid hallucinations, only I didn't find anything that said a person would hallucinate beyond their knowledge. How did I dream of hearing words I've never heard before?

The only reference I found to the word *Seelie* came from an old ballad for children. It was a fairytale-type song that said a queen of the Seelie Court turned a man back into his true form after a witch cursed him for denying her advances. From there, I looked for any reference to Unseelie but came up short. The term wasn't even used in any children's story that I could find, and the song mentioning the Seelie queen didn't go into much detail about who or what she was. I can only assume she was meant to embody either a good witch or a fairy godmother, and therefore *Un*seelie would be a wicked witch or evil stepmother. But Keela's family, the Vasilises, spoke these terms as if they represented real people. Witches are not real. They're old hags in stories meant to scare children. Or princesses. My parents weren't into the whole storybook prince and princess thing so I don't have a background in fairytales, but I do know that good or bad, witches are *not* real.

I check my phone. Collin still hasn't responded to any of my messages. He goes off grid on occasion, but usually only during school breaks and never without telling me his plans first. With the strange way Leah is acting and all the things going on inside my head right now, I need to talk to him.

"Hey." Gelby plops into the seat next to mine in the lecture hall, his sudden appearance making me jump. He lowers his voice and leans toward me with wiggling eyebrows. "Did you and Leah MacKenzie have a good night?"

I run a hand up along the back of my scalp, noting again that if I fell outside his house and on the stone sidewalk, so there should at least be a sore spot if not a lump. Just like the sore spot I got last night when Keela tossed me into the wall. It hurt when I first tried to get comfortable in my truck but now I don't feel anything. "Leah's nose is fine. Thanks for asking."

He groans. "It would take more than a busted nose for Leah not to be fine. And I mean that in more ways than one."

"Then maybe you should have been the one to take her—" I choke on my own air, breathing feeling like too much for my lungs to accomplish as my eyes land on Keela. She's in tight black pants and a soft blue top, and she's strolling across the front of the lecture hall in strides long enough to keep up with the much taller Rohan, who's walking beside her.

Gelby slams a hand against my back. Hard. "Breathe, and find someplace else to look because that's my sister you're staring at that way, and I don't want to have to dismember you before the end of our first day."

I snap my attention around to face him, Leah's warning about his family being dangerous at the front of my mind. Gelby smiles. "Relax, I'm only joking." I let out the air trapped in my lungs and focus back on Keela, who is taking a seat on the opposite side of the room, near the windows. "Mostly," Gelby grumbles.

I make a feeble attempt to roll up my tongue, straightening my posture and still failing to breathe properly. No one should be allowed to have this kind of effect on another human being. Especially when three murderous brothers are involved. "Class is half over so why are you guys just showing up now? All of you can't be freshmen."

He scans his siblings. "We can be many things, but you, my friend, only need to remember one golden rule." He leans toward me. "When you look at my sister, all you should see is a great big no-fly zone. Got it?"

Anger boils inside me. "No, actually, I don't get the overprotectiveness. I'm not going to hurt her or do anything she wouldn't want me to do, and she looks plenty old enough to make her own decisions."

He chuckles. "Yeah, she is. Which is the problem. For you, not me. Trust me when I say I'm only trying to help you."

I snort dismissively. "Whatever. I don't date sisters of friends anyway, so if we're friends, she's off limits automatically."

He slaps me on the back again. Harder than before. "That's the spirit. Fake it 'til you make it. You'll eventually meet a nice girl to settle down with. What about that one over there? She's pretty."

I right myself in my seat and don't bother looking where he's pointing. "If that's your type, you should ask her out."

The rumble of Haldir's voice so close to the back of my head startles me. "Gelby's type usually has a little more fur. Smells up the whole house when he brings a date home."

Gelby leans back and glares at his brother. "At least I can get a date."

Haldir lets out a huff. "Getting a date is easy, and unlike you, I don't do easy."

Both of them jump to their feet and I shake my head. "This is why I'm glad I never had a brother. Your stupid sibling rivalry is going to get us all kicked out of class."

Gelby grips my elbow and despite my best efforts, I can't shake him. He drags me to my feet. I glare at him. "I don't fight over girls but if you really want to do this, let's take it out of your sister's sight because I don't want her getting upset when I put both of you in your place."

Gelby is ignoring me. He's locked into Haldir and I glance between them. The brothers are having a conversation with their eyes, and I hope it's one that is going to tame their egos. Gelby's head shakes. "Bishop isn't going to like this."

Haldir nods once. "Get him out of here, or else I might dismember him myself."

"Wait. What?" I exclaim as Gelby drags me past Haldir. I crane my neck to look behind me. A few people are staring at us but most are averting their eyes, including the professor who despite looking mildly put out by the disruption, isn't bothering to directly acknowledge it. A boom rattles the walls. The window beside Keela shatters and she hits the floor. Screams fill the air and a shout rips from my own throat. "Keela!"

Gelby whirls me around and shoves me out the door. "She can take care of herself."

I try to spin back into the room but the chaotic stream of stampeding students emptying out of the lecture hall only shoves me farther away. I swing my arms against the flow, trying to scatter the terrified students as I press my way back to the room. An arm wraps around my throat. "Don't make me do this the hard way." Gelby drags me backward. I claw at his choking grip until my dilated eyes focus on a swirling mass of darkness slithering over the walls and up along the ceiling.

I stop clawing and instead tap on Gelby's arm, making a choking sound when trying to speak. "Oh, for Álfar sakes," he mutters, the words spewing out like a curse. His chokehold loosens but he doesn't stop moving. "You're going to want to cover your nose."

I buck against his grip just as the odor of rotting roadkill fills my nose. A raccoon was run over outside of my house one time, and it took all of thirty-six hours for that thing to stink so bad Mom begged me to shovel it off the road and bury it. What I'm smelling right now is so much worse. I gag. "What is that smell?"

"Draugr," Gelby answers.

"Dra...what?"

He releases me and shoves me behind him, pointing at the three figures lobbing up the hallway just behind the swirling plumes of darkness. "In short, zombies."

I rub at my throat. "No. No way. You people are messing with me and this isn't funny anymore. You're going to get someone hurt."

He shakes his head at me. "Humans."

I point at the dark trio dragging up the hallway toward us, and all the screaming students darting around trying to avoid them. "Yeah, humans. You're freaking everybody out and we just left your sister in that room to get showered in glass."

He flips his palms face up at his sides. Two glowing orbs of electricity materialize above his hands, sparking in cords of blue just like the vines that encased me in the void. I stumble away from him. He launches an orb. It explodes at the feet of the zombies, shooting a sizzling wall of electricity straight up to the ceiling. He launches the other orb. It hits at the far side of the door to the room Keela is in, forming yet another sizzling barrier. The grotesque humanoid creatures beyond the first wall begin to morph, growing larger, with sharp teeth snapping out of their now massive jaws. I point a shaky finger at them. "Are those sabertooth tigers?"

Gelby gives me a nervous smile. "Did I forget to mention these zombies are shapeshifters?" I nod stupidly, watching the beasts gnash and claw at the first wall. They slice through the thick vines of electricity, hacking away at the first wall until the plume of shadowy, slithering darkness makes its way through and spreads across the face of the second wall. "Yeah, well, I was little more worried about the Jötnar. That's the black swirly smoke. The Draugr will eat you, but these particular Jötnar devour you. Soul and all. It's best not to tick them off."

I swallow, heart racing. "Who exactly ticked them off?"

He shrugs as his first wall fully crumbles and the Draugr slam into the second. "I don't really like to point the finger of blame, so just run."

One of the beasts grabs hold of a vine and shakes its massive head, snapping the electric cord. A thread of black smoke begins to bleed through the wall, materializing into a solid form. Gelby turns and shoves me. "Now. Running tomorrow is going to be too late, dude."

I kick myself into gear and race down the hallway beside him, chanting, "This isn't happening. This isn't happening."

Gelby darts around a corner and watches the hallway behind us. I stop running. "What is it? What's happening?"

He lets out another string of what sounds like curses, only in a language I've never heard. Gelby throws another blue ball of lightning and then shoves me back into a run. "The good news is, I don't think they're here for you. We're not going to stick around to find out but I think they're here for Keela."

I plant my feet, my momentum making me tumble head over heels. I faceplant into the wall. Gelby glares at me. "I know you're human and all, but running is simply putting one foot in front of the other. How hard can it be?"

I peel myself off the floor. "We have to go back for her."

He huffs. "*We* need to do nothing other than get the fragile human to safety."

I tap at my chest. "Me, right? I'm the only fragile human because none of the rest of you are anything close to human! You're...things that walk through fireplaces and throw balls of lightning."

He crosses his arms. "We're not *things*, we're people. Just not human ones."

I march past him. "Well, this fragile human wants to go back for your sister. Be a coward and keep running if you want to, but I'm not leaving her." A deafening screech echoes down the hall, followed by an inhuman roar that vibrates the tile underneath our feet. I shudder. "What in the hell was that?"

Gelby waves his hand through the air. A trail of electricity follows his fingers until the burning edges of an oval just like the one I saw Aether dive out of stands in front of us. "Bishop refused to turn Keela over to the Unseelie for questioning. I'm guessing the Unseelie decided to retrieve her on their own." He slams his hands against my arms. "That noise is my family letting the Fae know that if they want Keela, they'll have to send an army larger than this one." He dives into the center of the glowing oval, dragging me with him. The world goes dark and I scream, but all I hear is the blood rushing through my ears.

15

I sit on the edge of the leather sofa and dip my head into my hands. My stomach is whirling, tilting, flipping end over end like I'm on one of those sickening rides Collin used to force me onto at the carnival. He couldn't get enough of the puke-eliciting rides and by the end of the night, he'd be screaming with laughter while I was bent over the nearest trash can.

Gelby bumps my knuckles with a can of ginger ale. "Portaling gets easier the more you do it. Sip on this and you should feel better soon."

I lift my head and smack the can away. "I don't want a drink. I want an explanation. Portals? Fae? *Zombies?*" I look past him to the normal-looking fireplace that I'm now fairly certain I walked into. "What's happening? Who are you, and how in the hell did you wave your hand in the air and poof, we're in your house instead of the hallway of the science building at Merrymont?"

He sits on the arm of the sofa, once again offering me the can of soda. "I didn't wave my hand through the air. I pulled power *from* the air and opened a door between where we were and where we are. As to the rest, we should wait for the others. Bishop and Rohan will decide what to do with you."

"Bishop?" I question. "He's the big Santa Claus-looking guy?"

Gelby chuckles. "Yes, Sean Winkle, and he knows if you've been naughty or nice."

I go to stand but my legs are still jelly, just like Santa's belly, so instead, I snatch the can of ginger ale from Gelby. "You're the one Santa needs to know about. You did something to me the night you walked me to my dorm. I was knocked out cold."

Gelby rubs his chin. "I don't recall hitting you."

I open the can and take a sip, my stomach thanking me. "No, you probably just had Keela *compel* me again." I tap my head. "Since you abandoned her to the soul eaters, I guess I'll never know exactly what she did to me. And what do you mean, Rohan and Bishop will decide what to do with me?"

The front door swings open and in marches Rohan. Followed by Keela. Haldir is on her heels, leaning forward and speaking directly into her ear. Gelby slaps me upside the head. "See there, she's perfectly fine. And you're staring again, which is a bad idea."

I drop my eyes but I hear part of Haldir's whispered words as they stomp past me. "Please, Keela. Let me do this for you."

My eyes find her legs, moving slowly up the curve of her calf to where a gash splits the fabric of her pants open. My fists clench at the sight of the blood oozing out of the back of her thigh. "You're hurt." I scan the rest of her bloody and torn clothing before turning to Gelby. "She needs a doctor. I'd take her to the hospital myself but you scrambled my head and I can't stand up yet. Do your portal thing and get her help."

He snaps his fingers and Keela's clothing knits itself back together, the stains, rips, and even the wrinkles. The same goes for Rohan and Haldir, who looked much the same as Keela, only without the leg wound. I stare at their clean, crisp clothes. "How…?"

Gelby lifts himself off the arm of the sofa. "Magic, bro."

Rohan circles back and slaps Gelby upside the head, and I mark it down that this family likes that move, since Gelby did the exact same thing to me seconds ago. Gelby flips his palms over and I brace for the impact of his sizzling orbs, but he only produces one and tosses it from hand to hand before twirling it between his fingers. "We have bigger problems than my impressive magic skills being on display. The kid remembers Keela." He snuffs out his orb. "I think he remembers everything, and yeah, I checked, he's still human."

Just as suddenly as Gelby poofed us here, Rohan has me up and dangling by the throat. "Where is it?"

My toes stretch for the floor, oxygen levels dropping as his fingers dig into my skin. "Where's…what?"

"The talisman," he snarls.

I can't draw in enough air to answer him and Gelby's stunt with the portal has my body feeling too much like liquid to swing on Rohan. "Drop him," a booming voice orders.

Rohan does just that. I fall into a crumpled pile on the floor at his feet, gasping and wheezing. Just like Gelby, Rohan is much, much stronger than he appears. I roll onto my back, looking up at fuzzy red pants tucked into black boots. Above them, a protruding belly hidden behind a white shirt is being tickled by a long white beard. Santa rests his hands on his hips. "You, boy, what is your involvement with the MacKenzie pack?"

I rub at my throat. "Collin's family?"

He bends down, eyes glowing red. "Liam MacKenzie. What is he to you?"

I scramble backward until I hit the side of the sofa. Santa's eyes dim and he asks again. "What is your connection to the MacKenzie pack? Answer me, boy, and no one will hurt you."

I slowly push up off my back and move into a sitting position with the end of the sofa still behind me. I rub at my crushed throat. If this is them not hurting me, I'd really like to stay off this family's naughty list. "Liam MacKenzie is my best friend's dad."

"You seem very keen on repeatedly mentioning Collin is your friend, and we saw last night that you are very close to Leah." Rohan closes in on me again. "How is it that you have become so close to them? Is Liam a father to you?"

"Not biologically, but a father figure?" Gelby adds to the questions.

I look around the room. Haldir is in his usual place, standing in front of Keela, who is slightly off to the side behind him so she can see over his shoulder. Her expression is blank. I look back to Rohan. "Liam isn't anything to me other than my best friend's dad. He doesn't really speak to me and I don't bother talking to him. I'm not close to Leah, either. Collin is the only one I'm close to. I got his sister out of a bar fight last night because if I had a sister, that's what I would expect Collin to do for me."

Santa...Bishop tilts his head. "Why did you enroll at Merrymont University?"

I slide my knees up and tuck my elbows against them. "To get an education."

Gelby offers me a friendly smile. "In the exact same place as your *friend* Collin?"

I glare at him. "Yes."

He winks at me. "Though you're the same age as him, you chose to come to Merrymont in Collin's final year because despite your friendship, you now have a...feminine incentive to be here?"

My eyes dart to Keela. Is he making that statement because of her? No, probably because of Leah, but she doesn't even go to school here. She opted to skip college. I clear my throat. "I'm here now because I finally have the money to be here. The MacKenzies are loaded but I'm not, and no, I don't take money from them. I applied to Merrymont after I knew I'd have the money to pay for it on my own."

Gelby squats down in front of me. "Are you sure your sudden appearance has nothing to do with the fact that Leah MacKenzie just rented a home nearby?"

I lower my head and consider his words. I saw Leah in Richlands days before I came here. She was coming out of a store and I drove all the way to the other side of town for lunch so I didn't take any chances on running into her. "I don't know what Leah has to do with anything, but if she's renting a house around here, it's news to me."

He smirks. "That explains why you took her to your dorm last night instead of to her house. How did she like spending the night in that *tiny* bed of yours?"

"How did you know...?" My heart skips and I look at Keela. She thinks I spent the night with Leah. "I didn't follow Leah to this town and I have no idea what she does or doesn't like. I slept in my truck last night and she was gone when I went back to my room this morning."

Gelby titters. "What, no morning cuddles?"

I narrow my eyes at him. "I told her to be gone by this morning, and she was. I haven't seen her since but I didn't miss the fact that she landed a blow on you last night. She isn't a nice person but I've never seen her attack anyone unprovoked. Maybe I should be the one asking the questions here."

Gelby rubs his chin. "Don't worry, I'm going to have a chat with her about last night. Do you happen to know where she went when she left your cute little room?"

I try to keep my eyes from widening. Gelby has a crush on Leah, and he's jealous that I took her home last night. "You seem to know way more about her than I do."

"Answer the question," Bishop's voice booms.

I swallow. "I have no idea where Leah is. The day after I got here she showed up saying that her dad needed Collin to do something for him. Then Gelby and Haldir invited me to a bar where I happened to run into her. If it wasn't for that, I wouldn't have been anywhere near her last night, and I can guarantee you she wouldn't have been trying to get anywhere near me."

Santa looks at Keela. She moves around Haldir and nods. "His heart reads true but his smell does not. He's marked."

Evil Santa swivels back to me, complete with fiercely glowing eyes. "You let her bite you?"

I glance between him and Keela. "No. I... Why would Leah bite me?"

Gelby straightens and Rohan drags me back up off the floor. "You tell us. You're the one who stinks of dog."

He shoves me toward Keela. She catches me, spinning me around and ripping open my shirt. "Here. As I told you this morning, it's fresh but faint. Leah didn't bite him, she scored him."

I look over my shoulder. "Scored?"

Gelby walks over and yanks my tattered shirt off me, tugging me away from Keela at the same time. "Leah laced her nails and scratched you. I would count you lucky because when she scratches, that means it was fun, but what she did to you is the equivalent of being pissed on and that's just gross."

I spin in a circle, slapping at my back. "I knew that witch was up to something. Where is it? Where did she scratch me?"

Gelby stops me from spinning. "Relax. She didn't bite you so you're little love marks will wear off."

"Unless he lets her mark him again," Haldir says. I meet his stony eyes. They bore into me. "Is that how you got inside our home? The wolves helped you?"

My shoulders slump. "Wolves?"

Gelby shakes his head. "The kid is clueless. He tried to run back toward the Jötnar because he was worried about...his classmates." He gives me a look that says not to say Keela's name. "I can't sense any charms on him either, and no matter how much scent Leah pumps into him, that won't get him past the wards. Something else is going on here." He crosses the room. "Bishop, Keela can't compel him. Have you ever heard of a human resisting compulsion before?"

"Human?" I squeak, clearing my throat until I don't feel like there's a mouse caught in it. "Can someone explain to me what in the actual hell is going on right now?"

Keela frowns at me. "Sit down."

I walk to the sofa and plop onto the cushion I was on before Rohan manhandled me. Gelby sighs. "That wasn't compulsion, he's just doing what she said because he...he's *human*."

Bishop stares at me. "I've never heard of a human resisting her kind, but I have heard of wolves conspiring with the Unseelie. What do you know about the Fae, boy?"

"The what?" I glance at Keela. "Your kind?"

For the first time, I see concern cross her features. Concern for me. She steps toward me, her voice soft. "Where is your friend Collin? We'll get him for you and he'll help clear all of this up."

I swallow. "I don't know where he is. Leah said he was off running an errand for his dad and I haven't heard from Collin since he left."

She takes another step toward me. "What errand did Collin have to go do?"

I lose myself in the curve of her lips, willing to answer anything they ask. "I don't know. He didn't even tell me he was leaving, Leah did. She said he was going to be gone for a while."

Keela continues her slow approach. "He's your best friend but didn't speak to you about his plans?"

I shrug. "Sometimes we go a week or two without talking. His family takes a lot of trips and they're pretty private people, so they don't talk about their personal lives that much."

Rohan presses a hand to Keela's arm, keeping her from coming any closer to me. "Your best friend doesn't share his personal life with you?"

I throw up my hands. "He tells me things, but he doesn't sit around giving me the play-by-play of all his vacations. He can be obnoxious but he doesn't brag to me because he knows I won't go on a trip I can't pay my own way for, just like I wouldn't come to this school until I could pay my own way." I glance at Keela. "I'm broke now, by the way, but I don't plan to be a pauper my whole life."

She looks at Rohan in confusion. I sigh. I guess making a point of telling her I have very little to live on until after college isn't going to matter if her brothers are going to decapitate me for even looking at her. "Just tell me what Collin and Leah have to do with anything. Did their dad do something? Is that why Collin had to leave?"

Bishop places a hand on Keela's shoulder. She looks up at him. "I can detect no change in him. He believes everything he's saying."

Bishop nods. "Then let us see how the MacKenzie pack will answer. Rohan, take a small party and pay Liam MacKenzie a visit. Search for traces of Aether while you are there. Keela and your brothers will stay here until you return."

"Yes, Bishop." Rohan dips his head, walks toward the fireplace...and blinks out of existence.

I gasp, pointing at the wall of brick and stone that didn't grow as Rohan passed through it. "What did he just do? Did he shrink? Did he freaking shrink?"

Gelby whistles. "I forgot to mention that the kid also thinks you're Santa Claus. I wonder how he got that idea?"

Bishop pierces him with a look and then moves off to the side of the fireplace. "Come here, boy."

Gelby nods at me. "Yeah, he's talking to you. And you should address him as Bishop. Or Nick, if you're feeling friendly."

I lift from my cushioned seat, not entirely sure my legs are reliable enough to keep me standing for more than a couple of minutes. "Nick? As in St. Nicholas?"

Bishop chuckles, his belly shaking exactly like the bowls of Jell-O Grandma used to make for me. "I've had many names, son, but only my wife calls me Nick. And only when I've crossed her." He winks at me. "Go on, see if you can walk inside."

I approach him cautiously. "You want me to go into the fireplace?"

He beckons me forward. "You got in once before. Let us see how."

I straighten my spine as best I can, fully aware of Keela's presence. It's too late not to look weak in front of her, I don't want to also appear to be a coward. "I don't know how I got inside before. The opening to the cave was wider. Taller. I just walked in."

Keela and Haldir flank me. I choose to look at her. She lifts a perfectly sculpted brow. "Cave?"

I cast a glance at the fireplace that isn't growing in size the way it did before. "The opening was big. Not like it is now. I didn't have to crawl, I just walked in." I look back at her. "The air inside is cool, so it has to be some sort of a cave. Right?"

Her head tilts. "How did you make it open for you?"

I shrug, ready to do anything but tell them I saw the thing grow before my eyes. Haldir grabs my hand and slams it against the stone mantel. The fireplace creaks and groans, its gaping maw opening as if to swallow me. I flinch away from it but he holds me in place. "He's using the runes. To do that, he needs magic."

"Or he's spelled," Gelby chimes in. "He's definitely human, so the question is, who spelled you, Sean Winkle?"

My already shaky legs beg to give out so I grip the mantel tightly. "There's no such thing as magic. There are no witches, and I don't care what my eyes are seeing, none of this is possible." I look to Keela for help.

"None of this is real. I'm dreaming, and I would prefer it to just be the two of us in this dream."

Haldir growls, Gelby pulls me away from the mantel, and Bishop walks past me. "Until we find out who spelled him and why we can't detect their magic, he stays with us. Show him to a room. I have an Unseelie Court to address." He turns and makes his way to Keela, pressing a gentle touch to her cheek. "The Jötnar came for you, not the boy, so stay with your brothers. I'll be back as soon as I can." He drops his hand and moves to the fireplace. In the blink of an eye, he disappears.

Haldir pulls Keela to him. "Gelby will see to the boy. You come with me. I will take care of you."

"No," she growls, stalking away from him.

Haldir surges toward her but Gelby shoves me at him. "I've got her. You take the wolf-lover to his room, and try not to kill him in the process."

16

The house is quiet. Haldir even more so. He hasn't said a word or moved a single muscle since Gelby and Keela disappeared up the sweeping staircase behind us. Thankfully I only bounced off his chest when Gelby threw me at his brother, so I'm not forced to stand here on my shaky legs. I backpedal to the sofa I was sitting on earlier and plop down. My limbs are getting stronger but I still need time to process what in the heck is happening, and time to figure out how to keep from being trapped here because it sounds like I'm not free to leave, and I'm hardly being treated like a welcomed guest.

I lean my elbows onto my knees and take a direct approach. "I don't know what room you're supposed to show me to but I'm glad we're on the same page about me not going there. All I want from you is a straight answer because so far, all you people are doing is dumping a whole lot of crap on me without bothering to explain any of it."

Haldir maintains his silence, standing so still I'm not entirely sure he's breathing. His eyes are fixed on the spot Keela was last in, his mouth shut, and his body rigid as stone. I clear my throat. "Things Gelby called *zombies* walked down the hall of Merrymont University today. I saw them with my own eyes. *Smelled* them. Then poof, I'm here, where fireplaces grow ten times their size. Start by explaining that to me. Why did it grow for me but San...Bishop and Rohan just...blinked into it?"

Haldir makes no attempt to answer. As much as my legs would prefer not to hold my weight right now, I force them back to standing. "Good talk. Maybe I'll see you around sometime, like when you're ready to give me the answers I deserve."

I square my shoulders and head for the door, throwing one last longing glance at the stairs. Despite knowing Gelby and Keela are up there somewhere, the house feels as empty as it did the first time I came here. I could go in search of them but I'm not sure what kind of *help* Keela needs. Gelby magicked away the gash on her leg, or at least I assume he did since he knit her clothing back together and she didn't seem to favor the leg when she ripped the back of my shirt open.

I grab the handle of the front door. It's locked. I check for the locking mechanism but there's nothing on, above, or below the handle. For that matter, there's no indication of a lock of any sort anywhere on the frame. Not a single latch, let alone a deadbolt. I try twisting the handle again, tugging with all my might. It doesn't budge. Up until today, I didn't think I needed to hit the gym any harder but now I know better. Gelby manhandled me and Rohan nearly flattened my neck. Neither of them even looked like they were exerting much effort either. If I manage to get out of this house, I'm prioritizing strength training.

"It's magically locked," Gelby's taunting tone makes me jump. "Don't let that stop you, though. I'm quite enjoying watching you attempt to break my magic."

I turn and face him. He's standing at the bottom of the stairs with his arms crossed. Keela is beside him, her hand resting on the railing. Her cheeks are flushed and her eyes are…dazzling. The whites are clear and the gold ring around her amber irises is so bright it seems to glow. I lift my hand and rest it against my chest. My heart is still beating so I haven't died and gone to heaven, but it's impossible to believe this woman could get any more beautiful, yet here she is doing just that. Haldir lets out a roar and Keela breaks eye contact with me. I drop my hand from my chest as she steps down onto the living room floor and crosses the room to Haldir. Only then do I look at him, stumbling backward and crashing against the door at the sight of the smoke billowing out of his nose. "What are you?" I rasp.

Gelby walks toward me. "He's angry."

The fireplace yawns open and Keela shoves Haldir into it. He disappears and she stomps in after him. The mortar creaks and the fireplace wheezes as it deflates back to its normal size. "What is happening?" I pull myself away from the door with hesitation. "How is any of this possible?"

Gelby drops his arms. "I'm sure you're seeing more than you ever bargained for, Sean Winkle, but let's get you some food. You're pale and you'll feel better after you eat." He turns and waves for me to follow him. "The kitchen here is stocked. I think. We don't eat much human food but there should be something here for you."

I unglue my feet from the floor and follow him, glancing nervously at the fireplace as we move through the octagonal room and pass under the balcony. "I don't want food. I want answers. I just spent fifteen minutes alone with a statue. Haldir could have been standing there dead for all I knew because I don't *know* how any of this works, or how it's even possible."

Gelby opens both doors of an oversized gray metallic refrigerator. "If Haldir was ignoring you, don't take it personally. He's not much of a talker. Unless it's to Keela. The two of them are close."

I lean against the marble-topped kitchen island. To me, Keela and Haldir don't seem *close*. He seems obsessed and overbearing, and she seems set on doing whatever it is she wants. "Will he hurt her?"

Gelby snorts. "Your concern is misplaced. Hal is the one you should be worried about. Keela is probably hurting him right about now." He tosses a package of sliced ham onto the countertop beside the refrigerator. "We should have some bread in that cabinet over there."

I cross the kitchen and open the pantry he pointed at. Not because I want to eat, but because I want to play nice. Leah is right about Gelby being the only one with decent manners. Keela probably does too, she just can't show it because of her brothers.

There are two dozen different types of bread lining the shelves. I grab the package closest to me. It's a bag of sweet rolls. "You're sure Keela's safe? Haldir had *smoke* coming out of his nose, like he's a walking campfire."

Gelby grabs a jar of mayo and picks up the ham, meeting me at the kitchen island. "I am as certain of Keela's safety as I am certain that you're going to get yourself hurt if you keep pining after my sister. You have no shot with her, Sean. Unlike Leah, it would appear."

I narrow my eyes on him. There's no way his remark was happenchance. He knows Leah dubbed me as No Shot Sean. "When I leave here, I'm going to hunt down Leah MacKenzie and I'll be sure to send her your love, right after she tells me what her part in all of this is."

He opens the bag of rolls and pulls a knife from a drawer in the island, cutting the roll in half and sliding the knife to me. "You think so little of Leah and yet she marked you as her property? I find that hard to believe."

I take the knife and hold onto it. "I find it hard to believe that anyone likes her, yet here you are, pining over Leah MacKenzie. Which makes me wonder if she didn't drag me into all of this just to make you angry because that girl is petty as hell. If the two of you are having a lover's spat and she thinks doing this marking thing on me will make you jealous, that's incentive enough for her."

He retrieves another knife from the drawer and slathers mayonnaise over his bread. "I doubt Leah marked you for my benefit, or for my sister's since Keela is no more interested in you than Haldir is."

I point my knife at him. "It's bad enough that I had to run from soul eaters. I'm not going to stand here, locked inside this twisted house while you people assault me and then proceed to *insult* me over something that happened to my body without my knowledge. Or my consent, for that matter."

Gelby touches the tip of the knife. An electrical charge runs up into my arm, shocking me. I drop the knife. "I wasn't going to stab you. All I want is a straight answer, and you're the one who brought me here, so either answer my questions or un-magic your door and let me out of here."

He slides the sandwich he just made over to me and picks up my knife, cutting into another roll. "No can do, my friend. Bishop says you stay here, so here you stay. Now eat. You'll feel better once you get some food in your stomach."

I step away from the island. "I don't want food, I want answers. Outside of Bishop, you're the only one who speaks to me in complete sentences, and Bishop only seems interested in accusing my best friend's family of somehow being involved in whatever brought zombies to Merrymont. Which they aren't. Not Collin anyway. Leah is one of the worst people I know so she might have gotten herself mixed into all of this, but Collin didn't and *I* sure as hell didn't."

I take a deep breath and move back to the island, placing my hands palm down on the black marble top. "I feel like I'm losing my mind. What I've seen *can't* be real. Am I in a hospital room somewhere, deep in a coma? Or is this the apocalypse and all of you are biblical figures?" He chuckles. I drop my head. "See what I mean? I'm losing it, so just tell me in plain English whether or not all of you are hallucinations or if the world is ending because I'm here, in whatever this is, and not by my own choice."

He leans his forearms onto the island and frowns at me. "I am real, and that I know of, you are not hallucinating. As for my family, we may have inspired some of those biblical stories, but we are not angels. Ragnarök, your apocalypse, has not come to Midgard."

"Midgard?" I ask.

He sighs. "It is where we are. The human realm that you call Earth."

I swallow. "And you're not from Earth?"

He shakes his head and a shiver runs through me. "What are you?"

He lifts his forearms from the island and goes back to making another sandwich. "My family is not human, and humans are not supposed to know about us, hence the reason our manners are rusty." He takes a bite of his sandwich and nods to the one still on the counter. I pick it up and he grins. "We're not used to having one of you around. Generally, anyone we associate with knows about the whole world, not only your tiny human part of it. And in our world, secrets are kept at all costs, and information is costly."

I take a bite of the sandwich, hoping my compliance will keep him talking. My stomach growls and I realize I haven't eaten anything today. "Now that I know about you, what happens to me?"

He sighs. "Keela is a bit of a genealogy expert. She's been researching your family and so far, she's found no magical ties. But someone has spelled you, Sean. And not with simple run-of-the-mill magic. Whatever was used on you is powerful. Until we figure out what it is and why it was done, you stay with us."

I force my throat to work as I swallow down my second bite. "I'm a prisoner then? Not allowed to go back to my own life because someone did something to me that you guys don't like. And you think that someone is a MacKenzie? You think they brought those monsters to Merrymont today?"

He chuckles. "No, we aren't accusing the MacKenzie pack of bringing the Draugr or the Jötnar. It's unlikely the Ulfr would even know how to contact those races, let alone enter their realm. The Ulfr are watching *you*. And closely. That's why we're interested in them."

Watching me? It has to be Leah. Collin isn't even here. "Ulfr?"

Gelby walks backward until he's resting against the counter behind him. "What's important is that we were there today when the Draugr attacked. We felt the disturbance when they entered our territory and thought they might be coming after you. They weren't. It seems the Draugr were sent to distract us while the Jötnar fetched Keela. Which we also knew could be a possibility. Information I already gave you, and for free, I might add."

I rub at the part of my hand where the burn had originated from when I first saw Keela. It isn't burning now, but I feel a bone-deep ache. "Keela is in danger, then? Just not from Haldir."

Gelby laughs. "Using the Jötnar was a bold move, but they would have had to catch Keela alone to be anything close to effective. Since we expected some form of retaliation after Bishop told the Unseelie Court to take a hike, we made sure she wasn't alone. We also made sure to protect you." He stalks around the island and comes toward me. "We saw you staking out our house. Why did you come back here and attempt to break in for the second time?"

I put down my sandwich and roll my shoulders, not missing the fact that he isn't telling me exactly what kind of aliens they are. "I didn't break in the first time. I knocked and the door opened. I shouldn't have just walked in after that, but I did. Then, when I came back the next day, it was because I..."

"Remember everything," he finishes for me. "In your dorm room, I was able to knock you into a deep slumber, but Keela's compulsion isn't working on you. Whoever spelled you either knew you'd encounter beings with the ability to erase your memories, or they intended for you to. Since they also gave you the power to slip past my wards, I think you were meant to be here with us, Sean. Now all we have to do is figure out if you were sent as friend or foe."

I gape at him. "Friend. At least, I don't have any reason to be against any of you." My fists clench. "Well, Haldir is on thin ice with me but only because he seems to have put me on thin ice with himself."

Gelby's face hardens. "I think both of you are too much alike to be left in the same room together for too long, but I want to make something clear to you. I added wards to our house and since you couldn't get in the second time you came here, it seems that whoever sent you was familiar with my magic and yet they failed to expect that I would strengthen my family's defenses. That was a mistake on their part. My family will fight for each other until death. You may not like Haldir and he may not have spoken to you, but had your magic allowed you to escape this house today, he would have caught you before you made it off the porch."

My jaw clenches. "Because I'm a prisoner. One you intend to kill?"

His eyes move past me. "I intend to remove your magic. After that, Keela will compel you and you'll go back to your mortal life. In the meantime, if you attack any member of my family, your death will be swift." He shoves a hand out to his side and wiggles his fingers. "Go to Haldir. Tell him Arsenious is here."

I look around. "Who is Arsenious?"

Gelby's intense eyes glow an otherworldly blue. "He is the father of a missing friend and if he knows you were present when his son went missing, he will remove your head upon sight."

"Collin?" I say the name of the only missing person I know.

"Aether," Gelby corrects. "I've opened the doorway for you. Go. Now."

17

"Aether?" The name feels numb on my lips. "Arsenious is Aether's father?"

"Yes, "Gelby answers, his palms sizzling to life and electricity sparking through his eyes. He didn't look this fierce back at Merrymont. A shiver quakes through me. Arsenious is either worse than zombies and soul eaters, or Gelby on his own is no match for Aether's father. "Go," he grinds out. "The Fae spelling a human to start a war with us would not be a surprise, but if they have done this, Arsenious is here to hide their deeds. He *will* kill you on sight."

A pale blue gust of magic slams into my torso. I throw my arms out but it's too late. My body folds like a taco and before I get a chance to yell, I'm flat on back in front of the fireplace. It's already wide open and I don't think twice about scrambling inside as Gelby storms past me, heading for the front door. Cool air hits my face and I push my feet into a run, stumbling through the dim corridor in hopes of finding Haldir. I don't know what he is but if he has powers like Gelby, then Hal needs to be by his brother's side.

Unlike the last time I was encased by these stone walls, I hear the screech of tires echoing from the end of the tunnel instead of voices. I run toward the sound. The light. My thoughts racing right along with my feet. If I was present when Aether went missing, that means no one has seen him since he shoved his hand into my chest.

I round the corner and enter the billiards room. The large-screen television is displaying a racetrack. A pearl-yellow Ferrari cuts in front of a rubystone red Porsche, sending the latter spinning into a wall. "You'll pay for that, Keela," Haldir growls, the top of his head barely visible above the plush top of the gaming chair sitting only a few feet away from the television.

"You're the one who insisted that I play," Keela retorts.

His head turns toward her. "You have to do something other than sulk."

Her Ferrari crosses the finish line and she immediately gets out of her seat. "I'll stop sulking when you stop brooding. Until then, if you don't want to lose, play your little games with the human."

I lean my hands against the pool table. One of these days I'll find out how she knows I'm in the room without looking. Maybe it's my deodorant. I put it on thick this morning. "The human has a name, and Gelby needs Haldir." Neither of them respond or even bother to look at me. "Right now!" I add.

Keela slides onto a chair across the room and pulls a thick book onto her lap. I scan the table of books next to her. They look old and I wonder if they hold any of the answers I seek. I pull away from the table and march toward the gaming chairs. "Though I have nothing better to do since I'm a prisoner here, I'm going to pass on playing your video game. Take the loss Keela just handed you and go help your brother. Gelby didn't look too happy about Arsenious being here."

Haldir vaults over the chair but it's Keela's presence in front of me that shocks my tongue down my throat. I gape at her. "Did you just portal instead of walking ten steps?"

Her jaw clenches. "Arsenious is here? In this house?"

I wipe a hand over the back of my neck. "Yeah, and apparently he wants to kill me. Gelby is going all electrical storm over it."

An animalistic roar cuts through the room and hot steam boils against my face. I blink at Haldir. Smoke is billowing from his nose again, but it's his eyes that have me backing away. The whites are a flow of molten lava, red and orange flames licking at the edges of dark, slitted pupils. "What are you?" The words hang in the air as another roar escapes his chest.

"Stay." His deep voice sounds more animal than man, his order directed at Keela. She keeps her eyes on him as the beast moves past me. I reach a hand back toward the pool table to steady myself, feeling the shift in tension as Haldir leaves the room we're in. Not that his absence is making much of a difference. Keela is still wound tight as a bowstring. She's here, though, with me instead of out there with all of them.

I lift a shaky hand to my face, feeling the tremble in my fingers as I wipe the tacky steam from my chin. Forasmuch as I don't want to appear weak in front of Keela, even the hardness of her features is causing me to shiver. She's no more human than the rest of them. "What..." I clear my throat in hopes of keeping the shake out of it. "What is Haldir?"

Her fingers flex. "He didn't mean to scare you. Dreki are not known for their self-control, and Haldir sometimes forgets himself."

I glance at the mouth of the tunnel behind me. "Especially where you're concerned."

She remains glued to the spot she was in when Haldir ordered her to stay. "Dreki are protective and fiercely loyal. Haldir doesn't take kindly to uninvited guests in our home."

I wince at the remark, but I'm not going to defend my reason for walking into her house uninvited because Haldir isn't the only one losing his composure right now, and the only fight I'm up for is the one keeping me from losing my crap right here in front of her. "Since your...*brothers* aren't happy about Arsenious being here, I take it you weren't close to Aether's father?"

She stalks to where Rohan had been standing last time I was here and flicks her hand at the wall. It shimmers and disappears, leaving a glistening wall of weapons in its place. Her hand runs over a set of daggers. "If I find out the Fae King had anything to do with Aether's disappearance, I'm going to get *very* close to him."

"King?" I feel faint as she takes the daggers from their place and wraps her fists around the hilts. "What are Fae, Keela?" Maybe I can keep her talking and safe in here with me.

With hindered movements, as if she's unwilling to let go of the weapons yet is forcing herself to, she places the daggers back into their slots and flicks her hand at the wall again. It shimmers and is once more an unassuming slab of solid stone. I wipe my hands on my pants and lean forward, allowing my hands to mold to my knees for support. "You really aren't human, are you?"

She turns and paces back toward me, every few steps drawing her eyes from mine to the corridor leading back out to the main house. "You have found yourself in a place you shouldn't be, Sean Winkle."

I inhale deeply, grateful for the cool air around me. "I'm starting to think I have the worst luck a man could have." She opens her mouth and then closes it. It takes me a second to realize what an unsympathetic jerk I'm being. Human or not, her boyfriend is missing and I might want to kill him, but she cares about him, and I care about her. There's no point in denying that much. She might have compelled me or used some kind of magic to make me want to be her lap dog, but if I get to kiss that blood-red mouth of hers, I'm happy to be whatever she wants me to be. Which makes me hate myself a little bit.

I straighten and decide to ignore the topic of Aether because if I tell her I hope he comes back to her, I'll only be lying and Bishop acted as if she's some kind of lie detector. Plus, she's finally speaking to me. A subject change might help both of us out. She can put her mind on something other than Arsenious being here and I can get a few more answers. "I guess my luck could be worse. Thank you for revealing what Leah did to me. I still don't understand exactly what she did or why, but knowing she's up to something was worth losing a shirt over."

Her eyes scan my bare torso and I've never been more grateful for my gym membership. The other guys in school didn't have to work as hard as I did for this physique, but if Collin and the others hadn't been the studs they are, I probably wouldn't have been motivated enough to lift a single weight.

She looks away. "Gelby should have reclothed you. I don't have that magic or I'd do it myself."

I run a hand over my abs. Impressing her would almost make getting blasted with Gelby's magic worth it, but I can't tell if she likes what she saw or if I should try to cover myself up. I'm sure one of Rohan's shirts would fit me. "Um... Can you tell me exactly what it was that Leah did? Gelby makes it sound like it's something intimate, but Leah and I have never been close. We don't like each other, especially in that kind of way."

Keela smirks, one corner of her perfectly formed lips ticking up. "I heard you have no shot, Sean."

My eyes narrow of their own volition. "Yeah, it seems everyone has heard that."

She smiles and I feel that smile all the way to my very core. Peace settles over me and I smile back at her. She looks away, her lips falling back to their natural unsmiling state. The hard set of her jaw reminds me of Haldir and I scrub both my hands up my face, trying to forget the fire in his demonic eyes. That has to be what a Dreki is. A demon. "I was very young when I had a crush on Leah and it didn't last long. Since then, I haven't wanted a shot with her any more than she wants to give me one. Which is why I'm confused. I barely see her, let alone speak to her."

Keela paces toward the corridor that leads back to the main house. I follow her. Whatever is happening with Arsenious, Haldir wants her nowhere near it and I don't either. I need to keep her from charging down this tunnel. If I can do that while also pleading my case and letting her know that I'm not romantically involved with Leah, that's what I'm going to do. "It was weird that Leah showed up in my dorm but I didn't think too much of it. Now I'm stuck in this place and hearing about being spelled, and marked, and seeing things my own eyes don't believe." I push my luck and place my hand on Keela's shoulder. "Gelby called Leah an Ulfr. Do you know what that is?"

Keela stops at the mouth of the corridor. "Leah and her whole family are Ulfr. What you might understand as beings who can shapeshift into wolves."

I gasp and she looks at me, her eyes dropping to the base of my neck, just above my collar bone. "The Ulfr maintain human form most of the time and therefore live as humans do, but they have a society all their own. With customs, rules, and traditions." Her eyes lift back to mine. "So yes, Sean Winkle, it is *weird* that she marked you as her mate when you are not Ulfr."

I let out a breath and Keela does the opposite, drawing the air into her lungs. She takes a step toward me, her eyes burning into mine. "I will find out what your wolf is up to. The same as I will find out where Aether is. Stay here. You seem prone to finding yourself entangled with the wrong people and the only right thing about Arsenious is Aether."

She marches into the corridor and it takes me a second to recover from the fierceness of her stare. "Keela, wait." I catch up with her. "Haldir told you to wait and with the way Gelby forced me in here, I imagine he doesn't want you around Arsenious any more than Haldir does." She doesn't respond and the farther we walk, the more tense I become. I let my arms swing at my sides, my fingers aching to brush against hers. "I'll support your decision here, but are you sure this is a good idea?"

She stops. A smile spreads over my lips but it's short-lived. I didn't notice before, but there are markings etched into the stone on either side of us. Keela waves her hand over them and instead of looking at stone, I can suddenly see into the living room. She snaps her fingers over her left hand and then pulls on the air above it, as if she's summoning something from her palm. She flicks her fingers forward and then blows. The scene in front of us changes and we are no longer looking into the living room. Instead, we're zoomed in on the formal dining room beyond it. There's a long wooden table flanked by a dozen ornately carved high-back chairs. Gelby is seated in one of them, his face unreadable as he stares at the silver-haired man sitting across the table from him. Like his son, Arsenious is strikingly attractive. I look from him to Haldir who is standing off to Gelby's right, hands crossed in front of him and his eyes back to normal. There's no question as to what he's thinking, though. If Arsenious makes one wrong move, Haldir will end him.

I step closer to the wall. "That's Aether's father? He doesn't look much older than his son."

A muscle in her jaw ticks. "Immortals age slowly. It's impossible to know how old they are."

I scrub both hands up and down my face. "Immortals. Great. As much as I love the fact that we're finally having a conversation, I really hope I wake up tomorrow to find out I'm a coma survivor."

She bends over and tugs a long-bladed knife from her boot. "If you wouldn't fight my compulsion, there would be no need for a coma." She faces me. "You have a bad habit of following me. If you do that now, you will die." She presses the tip of her blade to my jugular. "Stay here. My magic will allow you to watch what is happening and no matter what you see, do not move from this spot until Arsenious is gone from this house." She brushes against me, her eyes dilating. "Do not let your blood spill, Sean Winkle."

My pulse races at her nearness. I ignore the knife at my throat and reach for her but my hands collide with nothing but air. She's gone. I snap my eyes to the scene in the dining room. Keela strolls into the room. Shadows pool at her feet as if gathering to greet her before spreading out to all the corners of the room, dimming the light as she walks closer to the table. Arsenious snarls at her confident approach, his eyes dropping to the knife she still wields. She stops on Gelby's left and slides the knife onto the table, the hilt facing Arsenious. "What an unpleasant surprise, Your Highness."

His lips draw over his teeth. "Do not speak condescendingly to me, you insolent child." His narrowed eyes flick to Gelby. "There will be no negotiation. The Seelie Court demands your pet be turned over for questioning. If she is guiltless, we will return her." His cold eyes lift back to Keela. "After we remove her obstinance."

Gelby doesn't take his eyes off the man. "Did you hear that, Keela? You're quite popular today, in demand with both the Seelie and Unseelie."

"Don't forget the Draugr," Haldir adds.

"Or the Jötnar." Keela cups the edge of the table and leans toward Arsenious. He recoils. She smiles. "Would you happen to know why the Jötnar and Draugr came to see me today? Perhaps you're working with the Unseelie?"

Arsenious remains leaning away from her, picking at nonexistent lint on his soft white shirt as if his uneasiness is evident to all of those around him. My hands itch to knock the smugness from his face. "Do not lump the Seelie in with the foul likes of the Unseelie. As you can see, I came here myself." He lowers his hands and lifts his chin, roaming his eyes between the three Vasilis before landing his cold stare back on Gelby. "Bishop speaks of diplomacy and now is his chance to prove to us all that he intends to abide by the treaties he himself helped to draft. This beloved pet of his was the last person to see my son. She must be brought to the court for questioning."

Keela straightens. "How do you know who last saw your son when you haven't ever been a part of his life?"

Arsenious rises from his chair. He's taller than Rohan but of a slender build. Haldir growls and Arsenious's eyes flash with a glow similar to what I saw in Gelby's earlier. "Do not threaten me, dragon. A father has a right to avenge his son." His stare moves back to Keela. "My son was selflessly doing his duty for his people and while that kept me from him, it did not keep the Unseelie from monitoring his movements. You should know that they watched his every move, and that includes the ones he made with you."

Jealousy rips through my gut. This is exactly why I didn't speak to Keela about Aether. I can't tell her that I hope she finds him and mean it. Gelby lifts from his seat. "Aether is aware of his duty and the spies operating in both of your Fae courts. As are we. Bishop is with the Unseelie now and I have no doubt he will call on you upon his return. Until then, you will make no demands of the Vasilis, and your threats against my sister will end now."

"Sister?" Arsenious spits. "She is not Vasilis and we will never honor her as such." His face contorts with disgust as he looks at Keela. "Your kind is nothing more than a parasite and you *will* come with me to answer for your crimes against my son."

Gelby reaches out and places a hand on Keela's arm, as if stilling her from moving. "Crimes? You accuse our *sister* of crimes?"

Arsenious tugs at the cuffs of his linen shirt. "Not formally. *Yet.* But my son had no reason to be in this realm aside from her. Aether's trip was not sanctioned by the Unseelie Court, and we're all aware that the only time Aether left on unsanctioned business was to come here to see *her*. We know he was here."

Gelby nods. "Aether was here. We have confirmed that with both courts and we have offered our assistance in helping to locate him. What we will never do is turn our *sister* over to you. Now go in peace and return to your court with news from the Vasilis. We do not start wars. We end them."

I watch in horror as Arsenious's next words bring Keela to her knees. "Aether is dead." He pulls a small oblong box from his pocket and shoves it across the table to Gelby. "His body parts have been delivered to us." He looks at Keela kneeling on the floor. "One. By. One. All of them drained of blood. If attention is what this thing you call a sister wants, mine is now undivided." Arsenious turns away from the table. "Tell Bishop I expect his ward to be in my charge by the week's end."

Gelby helps Keela to her feet. "Arsenious." Her voice quivers, laced with a lethal undertone. "I will pay my respects to your son, and you will pay with your own blood if you had anything to do with Aether's death."

18

I press my body against the stone wall, leaning on its strength to support my weight. *Aether is dead.* I draw a breath of cool air into my aching lungs, remembering the voice in my head telling me to kill him. I lift a hand to my chest. When Aether lunged out of the portal and plunged his hand into my chest, it wasn't his death I was thinking of. It was my own life I feared for. Then the world went dark. I don't know what happened to Aether but I might have been the last person to see him alive. Or one of them, anyway.

I watch the far wall where Keela's magic is flickering, giving me glimpses of the shadows now clinging to her form as if they're living, breathing things come to comfort her. She's sitting at the table now, staring at the small box Arsenious dropped there before he left. I want to go to her, but what if I'm the one who killed Aether? Even accidentally and in self-defense, that's not something she'll forgive me for.

Haldir places a hand on her shoulder. "Looking will do you no good."

Gelby covers the box with his palm. "I'll do it."

"No." Her voice whispers through the room as if the shadows are carrying her word to the far corners in mournful repetition. There's so much pain in that one syllable. Despite the fact that Aether might have tried to kill me, and I most definitely didn't want him around Keela, I'd bring him back for her if I could.

I close my eyes. I can't choose this moment to be a coward. I need to go to her. I take another drag of cool air and open my eyes, pushing away from the wall. A shockwave slams me back against it. "Wielding your magic so openly?"

I try to force my head free of the punishing pressure but Rohan's magical grip is too strong. "I'm not wielding anything," I sputter. "Keela did this. Ask her."

His hand wraps around the back of my neck. "I will."

He slings me forward and I fall...through the vision Keela created, tumbling out onto the living room floor near the fireplace. I shove up to my knees. "I'm really tired of being pushed around. If you want to fight, Rohan, come at me fair. And yeah, that means *human* fair because that's what I am, and only a coward would bring magic to a fistfight."

Rohan leans over me. "Only a dead man would enter our home and attempt to deceive us."

"Rohan," Gelby calls to his brother. "Arsenious was here. He left a vision stone."

Rohan's attention narrows on his brother. "What vision?"

Gelby glances down to where I'm still kneeling on the floor. "Aether is dead. His body is...turned inside out."

For the hundredth time since I met this family, the air is too solid to drag into my lungs. I heard Arsenious say his son was delivered to him piece by piece, but what kind of monster turns someone inside out? Not me. I might have wanted to tear him apart limb by limb but how would I have delivered him to his dad? That means it couldn't have been me. I didn't kill him.

Rohan walks away with Gelby and I lift off the floor, trailing a few paces behind them. My whole body shudders when I see Keela sitting at the table, her upper body curled over her cupped hands where a soft yellow glow is illuminating drops of dark liquid. Haldir is on the floor next to her, chest heaving and forehead resting against her thigh. Gelby places a hand on Rohan's shoulder. "I asked her not to look."

Rohan's stiff demeanor sloughs off and he walks slowly toward his sister, lightly leaning over her and placing one big palm over her hands. "It is enough, *mia mel*."

She looks up at him, blood-red streaks running down her face. I race toward her. The dark droplets on the table are her blood. "Keela—"

"Back!" Haldir roars, his eyes aflame and his posture rigid as he rises from his place at her side to tower over me like the beast that he is.

Gelby throws a wall of electricity between Haldir and me, just like the one he used back at Merrymont. "Keela has lost someone who meant a great deal to her. The rest of us *will* control ourselves."

She stands, releasing the smooth crystal from between her palms. It bounces over the table and comes to rest against the box it was delivered in. "May you worship in Valhǫll, Aether. I will join you soon."

All three brothers take a sharp breath but only Haldir follows Keela from the room. I look to Gelby for answers. "What is Valholl?"

He lets out a tired breath. "It is the hall of the slain."

I whip my head toward the living room. "What is she planning to do? We have to stop her!"

"She will not enter battle alone." Rohan's words crawl over me like ice. "And you will not leave this place without telling us what you know of Aether's death."

I look between the brothers but I see no sympathy in Gelby as he moves to stand at his brother's shoulder. "I just found out all of you existed, so you tell me what kind of creature rips a man up and turns him inside out?" I look at the crystal on the table. "Is that truly what happened? And Keela saw it when she held that stone?"

Gelby's head dips. "Inside the crystal is Arsenious's memories of finding his son's body parts scattered all over Seelie." He looks at Rohan. "I looked for myself to see what Keela was seeing. It was a scavenger hunt. A grotesque yet bloodless one."

"Bloodless?" Rohan asks.

"Aether was drained," Gelby answers.

I press a hand to my suddenly upset stomach. I may understand the pain of loss but I never had to experience seeing my loved ones mutilated. "No one seems to trust Arsenious. Could he have hoaxed this to make you turn Keela over to him? He seemed set on getting his hands on her."

"Much like you." The hard edge of Rohan's voice makes his words sound like a threat instead of a statement. "The stone will not carry an untruth but your human tongue will lie with ease. I found no trace of Aether on MacKenzie land, but I also found little trace of your friend Collin. Tell me where he is."

I toss my hands. "I already told you that I don't know where he is, and Keela confirmed I wasn't lying, so instead of asking me the same question over and over, ask Liam MacKenzie where his son is. He keeps tabs on all of his family, even the nieces and nephews, so talk to him because I just found out ten minutes ago that they're...not human. The same as none of you are human."

A surge of power crackles through the room. "That's right." Rohan's hair begins to lift from around his shoulders. "I am not human, and while the MacKenzie pack is feigning the same kind of ignorance that you are, I have no treaty to abide by with you as I do them." Instead of hitting me with a dose of his magic, the power of it evaporates and Rohan uses brute strength coupled with the element of surprise to pin me against the dining room wall, his forearm digging into my throat. "Tell me what you know of Aether."

"I didn't kill him!" I grind without trying to fight back.

Gelby folds his arms over his chest. "You show up on the day Aether disappears, spelled, and unable to be compelled. None of those things are a coincidence. We know you saw Aether in the woods with Keela, and you have an unnatural wish to be near her."

"You *are* involved in what happened to Aether," Rohan accuses.

I have a flash of Aether's amused eyes as he kissed Keela. Then of his determined ones as he lunged from the portal on the front lawn. There was something else in his features, too. Something I didn't notice before because by that point I was already coming unglued. Aether was afraid. Doubt shivers along my spine and I clench my fists at my sides, tensing my muscles so Rohan can't feel the fear welling up inside of me. Now that I'm being held captive here, I don't know if it's safe for me to tell them what Aether did to me. I don't know if it's safe to tell them anything more than they already know. "I didn't know his name until all of you said it, but yeah, I did see him kissing Keela. Then she compelled me and it must have worked for a little while because I didn't know who she was when I saw her again. I just felt the need to follow her, so I did."

Their scrutiny tells me they aren't ready to believe anything I'm saying. I'm spelled, whatever that means, and they're looking at me as an enemy because of it. I shift to get the weight of Rohan's arm off my vocal cords. "Look, I don't know anything about wards and magic. I followed Keela because I wanted to talk to her. I knocked, the door opened, and when I called out no one answered. I got worried. That's why I came into your house. I wasn't sneaking around and breaking in for the fun of it. I was checking on Keela. That's when I saw...the fireplace, or the cave, whatever it is. It was big and wide so I walked in. The next thing I know, Haldir is huffing smoke out his nose and your eyes were glowing." I glare at Rohan. "It was pretty clear you weren't human, so I ran."

Gelby walks closer. "That's a cute story, but you're hiding something from us." Electricity sparks along his arms. "It's a very bad idea to lie to us."

I do my best to swallow around the hard plank of Rohan's forearm. If I knew what this spelling thing was, I'd feel better about telling them I encountered Aether on their front lawn. It's unlikely that I accidentally killed him in self-defense, and even if I did, I wouldn't be capable of doing what was done to Aether. "On my way out of your house, I saw one of those portal things you opened at Merrymont," I tell Gelby. "I've never seen anything like that before but as I ran down your sidewalk, there it was right in front of me. Aether jumped out of it and I guess that's when I passed out because the last thing I remember before waking up with all of you standing over me is seeing Aether materialize out of thin air."

Gelby's narrowed eyes widen. "You saw Aether portal onto our lawn?"

I adjust again, taking a ragged breath. I'm not going to tell them Aether attacked me. That will only make them believe more strongly that I had something to do with his death. I haven't exactly been passive with them so they'll expect that I retaliated against Aether. "Yeah, I saw Keela's boyfriend step out of a portal but I didn't kill him. I was too busy passing out."

A jolt of something warm spreads through me. "Who sent you here?"

I grimace. "No one."

More warmth filters through me. Rohan's teeth clench. "Tell me, or I will be the one to turn *you* inside out."

Gelby walks ever closer, his eyes on mine. "Do you feel pain, Sean Winkle?"

"Yes," I answer.

"Now?" he asks.

I look between him and Rohan and straighten my shoulders as best I can. I really shouldn't unleash a mouthful on them, considering, but they're really ticking me off. "I'd rather be living out one of my fantasies with Keela right now, but no, I'm not in pain."

I taste the blood in my mouth before I see it splatter. Rohan draws back for his second punch and I'm helpless to stop it. He strikes hard and fast. My head slams into the wall and snaps back to collide with his fist again before he draws his knuckles away for yet another strike.

"Brother," Gelby chides, placing his hand on my forehead. The spot underneath his palm grows warm and needles begin to prick along my scalp, prodding and searching until one finds entrance into my skull. I groan as the needle digs through my brain. It wavers in one spot, spinning and burrowing, drilling down into the very heart of all of my senses. My limbs begin to tremble. I beg him to stop but no sound escapes me. All I can do is watch the blood as it drips from my busted face to splatter on the floor beneath me.

"Take him to a cell." Rohan releases me from the wall and my body slumps away from Gelby's touch. "We *will* break his magic, and then he will talk."

"A cell?" I rasp. Rohan stomps away from me, approaching the fireplace and blinking out of existence. Gelby drags me to my feet. I trip along beside him as he pulls me toward the living room, wiggling his fingers as he did before, opening the fireplace wide so we can walk inside. "Where are you taking me?" I ask. He marches along in silence, his iron grip eating into my arm. I don't know what pain he expected me to feel earlier, but I'm feeling a lot of it now. My entire head is pounding and my left eye hurts when I try to move it. The eye socket is probably fractured. "I need medical attention," I tell Gelby, who is acting as if he can't even hear me. We reach what I've dubbed the billiards room and I immediately search every part of it for Keela. She isn't here. No one is. Gelby tugs me toward the corridor to the left. As curious as I've been about where the other corridors lead, I have a feeling I no longer want to know. "You can at least let go of me. I'm not going to run. I've already tried to get the front door open, remember?"

He continues on in silence. I don't resist. I keep my pace steady with his, the floor underneath my feet angling downward, dipping and curving until my stomach sinks into my feet. The stone walls are narrowing and instead of being smooth, they're growing bumpy. All around us, the smell of damp earth mingles with that of decay. We round a turn and I catch my first glimpse of the cells. They're dark and cut into the stone itself, with thick iron bars crisscrossing the front of them. On my right, the cells are wide and tall. On the left, they're small and cramped. I peer into each one as we pass but I see nothing in the darkness eating up the interior of each cell.

My feet falter as we near an open door. Gelby yanks me forward and I rip my arm free of his grip, backing away from him. "You can't do this to me." The set of his jaw tells me he can and out of pure desperation, I turn and run, knowing I'll never make it. I have no choice, though. It's give up or make them use force, and I'll never give up the fight to live.

My feet pound over the hard stone, skidding to a halt when a creature materializes on the path ahead of me. It's four feet tall, with a pointy hat threaded down over the top of candle-like ears that taper up into sharp points. The lobes are wide and wrinkly, drooping down over the creature's shoulders to pool in thick folds against its sleeveless green jumpsuit. Thick, brawny arms extend out of the jumpsuit and hammerlike fists rest on a snug red cummerbund fitted with picks and knives that's stretched around the creature's hulking middle. On its feet are narrow red shoes that curl up like a cake roll at the end, but it isn't this creature's fashion or even his weapons that have me backing away. It's the double rows of razor-sharp teeth lining its upper and lower jaws.

"Alberich." Gelby finally speaks. "You have a new guest. No one is to speak to him. My brothers and I will be back to question him."

"Guest?" I spin around but Gelby is gone. I turn back to the creature. It takes a step forward. I take a step backward. The creature advances on me again. I retreat in matching steps. "You're not allowed to eat your guests, right?"

The thing opens its mouth, gnashing its teeth back together with a sickening crunch. "Run," a weak voice calls out. I look into the cell beside me but I can't see anything. "Alberich will shred the flesh from your bones, just as he's done to me." A bony hand reaches out of the darkness, chunks of meaty skin dangling from the bloody wrist. Vomit rises in my throat and I do the only thing I can. I stumble backward until I reach the cell with the open door. Alberich races toward me and I rush inside the cell, sliding the door closed. It snaps into place with a thud and I don't need to attempt to open it to know I'll find it locked. For now, I'm grateful to be inside this cage, iron bars separating me from the creature snarling on the other side. Thick blobs of drool drip from its teeth and I back away from the bars. All I can do now is hope Alberich doesn't know how to open my cell.

19

I sit with my bare back pressed to the cold stone wall, my eyes on the bars at the end of the small cell. It's hard to tell how much time has passed in a place like this but from here in the darkness, it feels like hours have ticked by since Alberich walked away. I tried calling out to the bony-handed stranger in the cell down from mine but there was no answer. The only sounds in this place come in the form of an occasional wail or groan, and the soft clinking of metal. I reach again for the steel rings bolted into the wall above and beside me. It isn't hard to imagine what these are for. The Vasilis family has people chained in the bowels of their cave.

My only solace is that my head and eye no longer hurt. I can feel the dried blood on my face but it's no longer dripping down my chest. "Hello?" I call out again, moving onto my hands and knees to once again cross the cell in a grid. It's easier to keep my bearings and memorize the layout of my cage while I'm on all fours rather than standing and walking through the pitch-blackness the way I did earlier. There's not much inside the cell but I still tripped over the low stone bench that I assume I'm supposed to use as a bed. It sits on the left-hand side of the cell with a raised edge trench that I assume is a latrine cut along the right-hand side of the room. Thankfully my foot caught on the lip of the latrine before I stepped into it earlier. It wasn't until I got down on my knees and ran my hands over the ledge, around the box-like structure, and down into the gaping hole in the center that I realized what I was touching. My hand was clean when I withdrew it and there's no stench emanating from the hole, but that's of little consolation.

I find the stone bench and once again smooth my hands over the narrow slab, checking for bedding or even a sheet to stave off the chill that's settling deep into my bones. There are no hinges or hidden cavities. I'm alone in this place with not even a shirt to use as a thin barrier between me and the cold. I sit back on my haunches. A tinkling sound cuts through the silence. It's far away and at first, I pass it off as more chains rattling from somewhere deep inside this prison. The sound grows louder, closer. It stops. Starts again. Stops. And grows nearer to the edge of my cell.

I scramble away from the bars and plaster myself against the back wall. The edge of a cart nudges into view. It's three levels high with a two-rung ladder attached to the side of the silver cart. A creature scrabbles up the ladder. It looks similar to Alberich but two feet shorter and its long dark hair gives me the impression this one is female. She's also draped in a long green coat with red trim around the bottom and around the cuffs of the sleeves that ride up to her elbows as her tiny hands latch onto a white sack tied at the top with golden cords. She tugs it from the cart and hops off the steps. When she faces the cell her eyes meet mine and she startles, as if not expecting to find anyone in here. Her cheeks flush and she mumbles strange words under her breath before pressing her hand to the iron bars. A portion of them melt away, creating a slot large enough for her to shove the sack through. I race forward but the slot disappears as if it was never there. I kneel down to put myself on an equal, unthreatening level with this doll-like creature. With a gentle smile, I press my hand to the bars, hoping she'll understand that I won't harm her. All I want is to be free. "Hi, I'm Sean."

Her long ears wiggle and her eyes widen, more strange words flooding from her lips. She races around her cart and hurriedly wheels it away. I flatten my face to the bars and try to see down the corridor. "Wait! Come back! I'm not going to hurt you!"

"The dwarf will not allow his people to speak to you," a hoarse voice croaks. "Unless the Vasilis allow it." He pauses. "They never allow it."

"But why?" I ask, following the direction of the voice as I move across the bars. This isn't the bony-hand person, it's someone new. "Why didn't you answer when I called out earlier?"

"Hush!" the voice snaps. "You will draw Alberich if you're lucky, worse if you are not."

"I've done nothing wrong," I plead. "I don't deserve to be here. Someone has to know that, they have to let me out of here."

Laughter bubbles out of the croaking throat, more giggling joining in from cells all around me. A shriek cuts above the din and suddenly the entire prison is silent again, except for the distinct sound of bones snapping and lips smacking. My stomach rolls at the thought of someone being ripped apart, their body providing Alberich's dinner.

That monster should be the one imprisoned. If anyone is capable of doing what was done to Aether, it's Alberich.

I drag the white sack away from the bars and nestle it into the corner at the edge of light's reach. It weighs almost nothing but if this prison is my new home, I should see what's inside. Keeping one eye on the hallway beyond my cell, I loosen the golden cords from the top of the bag, doing my best to make no noise at all. The instant the cords touch the floor, they disappear. I take a deep breath. Just yesterday, something vanishing before my eyes would have shocked me. Now, I'm not surprised in the least. I'm a long way from what I thought college would be like.

I let the sides of the sack drop down to reveal the contents. It disappears the same as the cordage did, leaving behind a change of clothes, a sub sandwich wrapped in plastic, an apple, a bottle of water, and a thin gray blanket. I move the food aside and look at the clothes. They're mine. Someone must have retrieved them from my dorm. I'm not sure if that's a good sign or if it means the Vasilis family has confiscated all of my things. They seem like the type of people who can make someone disappear, and it wouldn't take too much effort with someone like me. All of my family is gone and Collin is the only friend I have regular communication with. Everyone else, even girls I've dated and stayed in contact with, won't think it's strange if they never hear from me again. Everyone knew I'd probably never return to Richlands once I sold my parents' house and with Keela's power of compulsion, she can erase me from the memory of anyone who might bother to seek me out. Unless they're spelled, like me.

I pull the dark blue t-shirt over my head and lean my back against the wall. It isn't much but the thin fabric does help with the chill. I lift the sandwich and slowly unwrap it, mindful of the noise, and of how quiet the cells are. I guess knowing the prison guard will eat you alive is a good deterrent. I only wish I knew if I could trust my stomach to hold down this food because I certainly can't trust anyone in the Vasilis family. This sandwich could be poisoned. So what if it is? I'm not a quitter and I won't stop fighting to survive this, but fighting feels moot at this point. Rohan stopped using his magic on me earlier but even then, my strength was no match for his. When it comes to my escape from this place—if I can manage to get out of this cell—I hardly think they'll fight fair when it comes to recapturing me. I'm a prisoner here for as long as they want me to be.

I lift the top of the bread from the sandwich and hold it closer to the faint light from the hallway. It looks and smells like roast beef. My stomach growls at the same time as it violently rolls. I set the sandwich aside. I can't fathom eating that without being certain the meat is meant for human consumption instead of being *from* a human. I pick up the apple and take a cautious bite. It looks like an apple and tastes like an apple, so I can only hope it is an apple. One devoid of poison.

Unsure of what to do with the apple core, I place it on the floor beside me and sure enough, it disappears. I guess this kind of magic would be cool if I wasn't trapped in a dungeon. I twist the cap off the water and take a cautious sip. It washes over my nearly empty stomach but more importantly, it tastes like plain water. That doesn't mean it is. The magic of this place could be making me think it's water when in reality it's battery acid. I take another small sip and then pour a tiny bit onto the edge of the blanket, using the dampness to wipe the dried blood from my face. I'm sure I didn't get it all but I don't want to waste the water. Who knows when I'll get more. Or *if* I'll get more.

I take another sip before considering what will happen if I put the bottle back down. I don't want to guzzle the contents any more than I want to lose what remains in the bottle. I slide the extra pair of jeans toward me and wrap the bottle inside of them to keep it from touching the floor. It doesn't disappear so I place the rolled jeans on the thin blanket and drag my meager bounty away from the small amount of light the hallway provides, returning to the darkness. I need sleep but I'm not curling up on the slab. Instead, I scoot into the corner behind it, place my jeans and water on the bench, and then prop my feet against the side of the slab, wrapping the blanket around my shoulders before leaning against the wall. I'm cramped in this space with my knees nearly tucked against my chest, but this is the best vantage point to keep watch on the bars of my cage. If someone, or something, comes inside, I'll be ready.

Metal scratches against stone. I try to sit up but I can't. Tremors shoot through my body and I convulse. "Again." Rohan's hard voice punches against the pain in my ribs.

"Any more might kill him." Gelby this time.

I pry my eyelids open. They're crusted and heavy as I look up into the faces of the three brothers. I'm still in my cell but no longer propped against the wall. I'm flat on my back with Rohan and Gelby kneeling on either side of me while Haldir stands at my feet. Rohan's hands are pressed against my abdomen and Gelby's palms are pressed to either side of my head. "What are you doing to me?" I hardly recognize my own voice. It's as hoarse as the one I heard from the other cell. My mouth and throat are parched, my lips pieces of driftwood at the edge of an endless desert. I try to speak again but my tongue is thick and heavy, unwilling to move. A bolt of electricity shoots through my core. "Rohan." Gelby removes his hands from me. "It isn't working and the boy is no good to us if he's dead."

Rohan rips his hands from me and climbs to his feet. "What kind of magic is powerful enough to resist us?"

Gelby runs a dry cloth over my sweat-soaked forehead. "I don't know, and I don't think he does either."

"I don't," I answer, managing to form words as I watch Haldir's eyes flicker against the light of the orb hanging in midair above his head. Rohan makes a dismissive sound, stomping away from me and out of the cell. Haldir gives me a hard look before following him. Gelby leans over me. "What do you know of enchantments, Sean Winkle?"

I close my eyes, wondering why all of them use my full name instead of just calling me Sean. Gelby pats my cheek. "Stay with me. If I can't extract the answers from you, you must tell them to me on your own."

I open my eyes, unwilling to speak to him even if my swollen mouth and cracked lips will cooperate. Gelby must see that truth in my eyes because he sighs and shuffles away from me, having a seat on the stone bench. "The memory crystal Keela held yesterday was enchanted." My heart thuds in my chest. *Yesterday? How long have I been asleep? How long have they been torturing me?*

"Other items can be enchanted as well," Gelby continues, rolling up his sleeves. "Gems, crystals, stones, sometimes even precious metals." He runs his finger along a raised scar that runs the length of his forearm. "Enchantments are used for many things and all Álfar adopt one or more for use in their wands." He smiles at me. "Not that we need them. The wands and the enchantments only amplify our inherent magical abilities. Each Álfr is born with gifts according to their heritage, and then we seek to become more powerful, learning to draw on magic within and without, imbuing our wands with enchantments and thus those wands become an extension of us." He pauses and I remain silent. He draws my attention to his raised scar. "Few Álfar do as I have done, but fewer still are as powerful as I am. Even my brother, the heir to our line, is no match for my magic." He traces the scar. "I have merged with my wand. Its enchantments course through my blood. Beat with my heart. Live inside my lungs, painting my very breath to make even the air I expel a weapon to be used against those who dare stand against us."

I run my scratchy tongue over the logs that are now my lips. "I'm not standing."

Gelby moves from the bench and snaps his fingers. A glass full of pebbled ice appears in his hand. He cups his hand under my aching head and lifts as he tilts the cup to my mouth. "There have been many centuries of war, Sean Winkle, and only in those times does anyone ever think about standing against us. We have been at peace for a long time now and until you showed up inside our sanctuary, we thought we still were."

As much as I don't want to take anything from him, my body feels as if it has been drained of all moisture. I greedily chew on a mouthful of the ice and bring a hand up to take the glass from Gelby. He gives it to me and helps to prop me back against the wall, staying crouched beside me while I throw back another mouthful of ice. "I'm sorry for what we did to you." He frowns at me. "My magic alone couldn't locate the enchantment buried within you, but there must be one. Spelled or not, a human cannot withstand what you have unless you merged with a very powerful enchantment."

I chew my ice and remain silent. I've already told them I have no idea what a spelling even is. Gelby adjusts his weight on his heels. "The first day you came here, Keela said you were human but we didn't believe her. That's why we didn't chase you. I checked for your magical signature and even without being able to find one, I threw out extra wards. Ones that should not have allowed you to escape. Any other creature would have been trapped in our home but somehow you walked right out the front door. By the time we realized you were escaping, I felt a powerful magical signature. I thought it came from you. Then we found you incapacitated on the lawn and we assumed my magic had reacted to yours, stopping you even though it was a little late to the party."

He straightens and paces the room. "We let you go because some enchantments self-destruct or return to a given location after they fulfill their purpose. We made the assumption that someone had used you. Therefore, we watched you, dug into your life, and tried to figure out who sent you here." He faces me. "It was Aether's power signature that hit on our front lawn. I cast a spell and tracked his life force. It ended there."

Gelby's eyes drill into me, searching inside me the same way his magic does. Though my every lash aches against my swollen eyelids, I hold his stare. Silently. His head tilts. "Do you understand what I'm telling you? Aether died on our front lawn, after encountering *you*."

He waits for my response but I don't give him one. He runs a hand down his face. "Aether should not have been able to portal here. Our wards prevent it and they're all still intact. There is evidence of a portal, though, so we know you're not lying about that part." He watches me for a reaction to his words. I give him nothing. He inhales deeply. "This home is protected not only by my magic, but by the magic of generations of Vasilis. We are impenetrable, Sean Winkle, and yet both Aether and you circumvented us on the same day, and now one of you is dead."

I cough, wincing over ribs that feel broken. "Talk to your Alberich, then. I hear he likes to eat people."

Gelby crosses to the front of the cell. "There are worse things in this realm than Alberich, and if you were in liege with Aether, whatever took him from us will most certainly come for you."

Days pass. I mark them by the delivery of my little white sack. There's never much food but I eat every morsel. Then I sleep. Ignore Gelby, Rohan, and even Haldir when they come. And sleep some more. I can feel my body weakening, and yet the pain and bruising from their brutal attacks wanes ever so slightly. It's as if the beast inside my head retreats further into my body, pulling my own consciousness down with him to protect my mind while we're under attack, yet he also somehow bleeds power into my physical body, protecting it from the worst, or at least mending my bones back together whenever the brothers use force to demand I tell them answers I do not have. They prod for information, Rohan playing bad cop while Gelby continues to build a fake friendship with me. Haldir stands at the cell door, a threat in his eyes. I don't care. Let them unleash him on me. They've taken everything from me and I already had so little.

I curl onto my side, numb to the hardness of the stone floor. Both from lying on it and from the cold still permeating this dungeon of a prison. Gelby left a warm light in the room for a while yesterday but when he returned, he found me ungrateful and snuffed it out, leaving me in darkness once again. From here, I watch Faralia's tiny feet scramble up the two steps of the ladder attached to her cart. I learned her name from Rohan. She came by once when they were attempting to torture information out of me and he barked at her, calling her by name when he told her to leave. "Hello again, Faralia," I whisper to her. She's still wary of me but she no longer flinches when I speak to her. Not that I ever say much. Alberich has come once more since I've been here and the gnashing that followed still haunts me.

Faralia presses her hand to the bars and I watch as the slot opens and she pushes the sack through to me. "Thank you," I whisper to her again, making no move to go for the bag. It didn't take long to realize it scares her when I move. The bars knit themselves back together and she stands there in front of them for a moment longer. I offer her a smile that I doubt she can see. I don't know what she is, but I'm grateful she has a humanlike face. It's round except for the point on the tip of her chin and her elongated nose. She smiles back at me and it takes everything within me not to race for the bars. I know I can't escape this place and I wouldn't endanger her by asking her to help me even if I thought I could, but I wouldn't turn away any information she could give me about where I am and what type of beings constitute all of the different names I've heard. Ulfr are shapeshifting wolves. Dreki are dragons. But I don't know what Fae and Álfr are.

As if she knows I'm thinking about approaching her, Faralia's pink face goes pale and her round eyes spread open until they consume half of her face. Her body trembles and a whimper escapes her tightly closed lips. I sit up. "Faralia, what's wrong?" A shadow passes over her and she begins to whimper more loudly. I use the stone bench to help me stand but before I can take a single step, Keela is here. She doesn't look my way. Her long legs walk her past my cell in short order. The instant she's gone, Faralia grabs her cart and hurries down the hall in the opposite direction. I rush to the bars, falling against them and wrapping my hands around the iron. I pull my face into the bars as tightly as I can, trying to see down the hallway. "Keela!" I shout, unable to see her.

Metal clinks and iron scrapes against stone. "Noooo," the hoarse voice moans. "Please, no." A moment later, there's nothing but silence. Dread trickles through me. I don't fully understand what Keela is but Faralia didn't tremble at the sight of Haldir, so Keela is something worse than a dragon. Still, I wait by the bars. There's something between us so if anyone can help me, it's her.

Keela's shadow moves through the corridor ahead of her. I swallow as it comes closer, remaining still as it passes by me, waiting for the woman herself to come into view. She does, and I shove myself closer, reaching my fingers through the bars. "Keela." She doesn't look at me and if I wait much longer, her steady stride will take her away from me. "Please," I rasp, so many things fighting for the chance to spill from my sore lips. "Don't hurt her." Concern for Faralia wins out. The little creature was terrified of Keela, whose booted feet are now still as they stand on the stone underneath them. My heart thuds when she moves with the agonizing slowness of a grace that only Keela can have. I hold my breath as I wait to meet her eyes. "Faralia was doing nothing wrong. Please don't let anyone hurt her because of me."

Keela wipes at a dark-colored smudge on the corner of her mouth. "Faralia?"

I pull my fingers back into the cell as she moves so close to the bars that my fingertips could brush against her body. I want to touch her more than anything but I'm at the mercy of her brothers, and of her. I can't do anything to upset the fragile thread I might have to freedom. "The...girl wasn't talking to me, I was the one speaking to her. She only delivered my bag." I motion to the sack that's still on the floor where it fell when Faralia pushed it through the bars.

Keela studies me. "How interesting. Leah MacKenzie will be devastated to know that her mate is so concerned about another."

I take a single step backward. "Why are you stuck on that? I am not Leah MacKenzie's anything, especially her *mate*. Whatever Leah did to me was without my knowledge. Is this why your family is starving and torturing me? To get back at her? Her family? Whatever they've done to get on your bad side, I had no part in it."

Her eyes scan my small cell. "We do not use pawns. If the MacKenzie pack crosses us, they will be the ones to suffer for their transgressions."

I scrub a hand over my mouth. "Then why does everyone keep bringing Leah into every conversation?"

Keela cocks a perfectly arched eyebrow at me. "You may not want to talk about her, but Leah MacKenzie most certainly wants to talk about you."

I move back to the bars. "Leah is here?"

Keela looks down at my hands gripping the bars so close to her waist. "Gelby is in contact with the Ulfr. It seems you are indeed intended to be her mate." Keela's eyes lift to mine. "It's unheard of for an Ulfr to mate with a human. Do you know what that means?"

I run a hand to the back of my neck, remembering Leah raking her nails down my back that day in my dorm. "I didn't even know she wasn't human until I met you, so no, I don't know what any of this means. I'm sitting here rotting in this cell and yet I can still hardly believe any of this is real." I take a breath to steady my nerves and shift closer to the bars. "If Leah is why I'm here, let me talk to her. I'll make her unmark me because I'll stay here until Alberich has picked his teeth clean with my bones before I'll ever bed Leah MacKenzie." I let my fingers stretch out to brush against Keela. "Help me. Please. You told Bishop I wasn't lying so you have to know I'm telling you the truth. I don't know anything about Ulfr or Álfar or magical enchantments." I curl my fingers against her waist. "I'm just a guy who saw a beautiful girl on his first day at college. I followed you, and I'm sorry for that, but stalking you is the only thing I did wrong. I don't know why you can't compel me, but trust me, I wish like hell that you could."

Her eyes darken and I feel her breath on my face. "Believe me, I wish I could too."

I rest my head on the bars and stare into her beautiful eyes. Sympathy bleeds into her features and she steps away, the fabric of her shirt brushing over my fingers as she removes herself from my feeble touch. "Alberich will not harm you, and you will not have to mate with the wolf if you do not want to." Her eyes dip. "You didn't know what she was doing because you are not Ulfr. During their mating rituals, their glands produce a serum that coats their claws. You would have smelled it if you were one of them."

"Serum?" I question.

Keela tucks her hands behind her back. "It's their scent, and it also numbs the wounds they create, for the most part, because to seal a mate bond, the wolves first scratch their partners. It's mutually done, and to a more severe degree than what Leah did to you. In fact, the marks she left on you are barely visible. She either did something to expedite your human healing abilities, or your spelling enhanced them. Whichever is the case, her scent on you is faint and her trivial claim to you will go away so long as you do not allow her to mark you again."

I tap on the bars keeping me in this cell. "Then I guess I should be thanking your brothers for keeping me safe from her, but that might break their concentration when they're torturing me for information that I don't have."

A muscle in her jaw ticks. "In the future, stick to sleeping with only humans, lest a wolf bites you at the height of your ecstasy and you find yourself sprouting fur. Though that fate would be better than some." She moves back to the bars. "Faralia isn't as innocent as she appears. Tempt her, and the Dvergr will enslave you."

"Enslave?" I gape. Keela turns on her heel and walks away. I shove my face back into the bars, wanting to soak in every last drop of her. "I don't deserve to be in here! Please, Keela! I'll do anything!" I shout after her. Two creatures who look similar to Faralia flatten themselves against bars of nearby cells as Keela strolls past them. Once she's too far down the corridor for me to see her, I remove my smushed face from my own bars. A minute later, the two beings scurry past. I trudge to the dark corner of my cell behind the stone bench and pull the thin gray blanket around my shoulders, slumping down to wedge myself once again between the wall and the bench I refuse to pretend is a bed. The two creatures come back by my cage. They're not alone. They're dragging a gray blanket with a white sheet draped over the lifeless body on the blanket. The hand flops out as they pass by and my pulse quickens. It's thin and blue, and I know in my gut that the dead body is that of the hoarse-voice prisoner.

I wait until the scuffling sound of them dragging the body through the corridor quiets and then I crawl back to the front of my cell and call out to the other prisoners. "We're all afraid, but please answer me. Call out your names so we'll know...if any more of us go missing. I'm Sean."

It takes a long time for any sound to answer me. When it comes, it isn't from one of my fellow prisoners. It's the footfall of Rohan, Haldir, and Gelby.

"No more." Keela's voice cuts through the agony screaming its way through my body. My seizing limbs relax and my head falls onto something soft.

"Aether died not only in our territory but on our front lawn, no less," Rohan's voice is stern with tension. "Bishop is answering to both the Seelie and Unseelie for this, Keela."

The softness under my head evaporates and I land on hard stone. If I wasn't already in agony, I'd care about that. It's the loss of my head nestled in Keela's lap that bothers me. I didn't know she was the softness until she took herself away from me. *Help me.* I beg the beast inside me. It isn't enough to be hearing Keela's voice right now, I need my body to heal so I can bring her back to me. "The Fae want *me* to answer for

178

Aether's death and I'm happy to do so, as I've told all of you. I did not kill him, and neither did this human."

"We know you didn't harm Aether," Gelby answers her softly. "What we don't know is how Aether was able to portal into our territory and how the human fits into what happened. The two of them could have been working together. Aether could have set this up and been the one to spell Sean, then something in their plan went wrong and now Aether is dead because of it."

"To what end?" Keela asks. "Aether had no reason to rise against us. Against me. Even if coerced he would give me a signal that something was coming."

A grunt that can only be Haldir answers her. "He called you away from us that day, and yet gave you nothing. Had we not followed you, he may not have sent the boy here."

Warmth spreads from deep inside my void, slowly billowing through my impotent limbs, mending and healing as it radiates through me. The sensation touches my face and I force my eyelids open. I'm no boy and as soon as I can stand up again, I'll prove that to Haldir. For now, I let my eyes track Keela as she moves to stand in front of the wall of muscle that is her jealous brother. "Had you not followed me, Aether would have told me whatever it was that he summoned me for to begin with. For him to risk the ramifications of using his magic on our property, whatever it was must have been urgent." She moves in a slow circle to look each of her brothers in the eye. "Now we'll never know because the three of you are arrogant and you made a poor choice on the day of Aether's death, just as you are making poor choices now." She moves back to me and lowers down, looking into my eyes with a pained expression. "We have no proof that he was spelled by Aether, and even if he was, I cannot, *will not*, believe that Aether meant us harm."

Rohan crouches beside her. "You trusted him, but he was Fae, Keela. Not even Aether would deny his own greed. That's why we *must* break this human's magic. We have to know the truth."

She nods slowly. "We must, but this is not the way."

"She's right," Gelby agrees. "He's healing faster than a human is capable of and that's the only sign of his magic. Even after weakening his human body, we've been ineffective in wearing down or even locating the magic inside of him. He is no different today than when we first began."

I want to laugh but it comes out as a sputtering mass of bloody spit. If they knew what I was feeling inside of me, they'd know that I'm nothing like I was when all of this first began. Keela's nostrils flare. She wipes the bloody goo from my face, leaving behind only the coppery taste on my tongue. Rohan gets to his feet. "Gelby, clean him up. I'm going to consult with Pete."

"Great," Gelby mutters, lifting his hand over my face.

"Don't." Keela pushes his hand away. "He's had enough of your magic. Let him shower and clean up on his own. I'll have Siomha send food for him." A gust of wind tickles my swollen cheeks and then Keela is gone.

Gelby sighs. "That's going to be a problem." Haldir makes a rumbling noise and Gelby shoves his hands under my arms. "Can you stand? If not, Hal will carry you."

My entire body feels gelatinous, like I'm nothing more than a festering bag of pus, but I'll wallow in my own filth before I let Haldir carry me. Or any of the rest of them, for that matter. I tuck my legs underneath me and don't bother trying to hide the pain as I keel sideways, away from

Gelby, and push up to my hands and knees. If I have to crawl out of this dungeon, so be it.

"Let us help you," Gelby insists, tugging me to my feet and wrapping my arm around his neck. Haldir moves to my other side and I jerk away but it's nothing more than a flinch. "Sleep," Gelby whispers. My head falls forward and before the dreams come, I feel weightless, as if I'm floating through air.

I sit on the edge of the bed, staring out at the courtyard surrounded by a ring of tall pines. I woke up on top of the quilt Grandma made for me but it's no longer in my dorm room. I'm inside the house I followed Keela to. The one Gelby dragged me through a portal to get to. I haven't even left this room and yet I know where I am. I'm not in the dungeon anymore but I'm still a prisoner in the big white house.

Two ravens sit in the branches of one of the pines, their beady eyes scanning the grounds the same way I am. Occasionally they call out and I wonder if they know how lucky they are. I'd give anything to be as free as they are right now, to be able to just soar away anytime I felt like it. Instead, I'm trapped inside a room with all of my things scattered around me. My meager supply of clothing is washed and hanging in the closet, and when I went into the marble-embellished bathroom earlier, I found all of my toiletries unpacked from the shower bag and arranged as if this is my house. It isn't, and I wish more than anything that I'd never sold my childhood home. I didn't need to attend an expensive college like Merrymont. I could have stayed where I was and kept following in Dad's footsteps at the car lot. "This is what ambition gets you," I tell the birds. They each cock their head to the side as if they can hear me through the glass and are trying to understand what I'm saying. One of them might be the bird that led me to Keela and if that's the case, I wonder what it thinks of the situation I'm in now. Did it know what she is? What her family would do to me?

I study the window. Even if it opens, I wouldn't be able to escape after jumping down to the grounds below. Gelby probably has some sort of magic surrounding the courtyard that will drag me back to the dungeon if I try to run away. Even if I could make it away from here, what would I do? Where would I go? I can take the money meant for my tuition and run with it, but the cash wouldn't last for too long. Then I'd be a drifter. One with a horde of monsters after me.

I look down at my hands. Thanks to my inner demon, I feel physically fine after the long shower washed away the bloody evidence of my torture, but my mind will never be what it was. While I'm grateful for the protection and the inhumanly fast speed at which my body can heal, I can't actually be considered human anymore. Not with this thing living inside of me. Collin isn't human, either. My best friend for all of these years isn't even the species I thought he was, and his sister violated me in ways I don't understand. I don't know how to bounce back from this. Even if the Vasilis let me go, I have nothing to *go* to. I might even be a murderer. I think it's highly unlikely that I had anything to do with Aether's death. Killing someone, even in self-defense, seems like something I would remember. Whether or not I was accidentally involved, Aether can't be the one who spelled me. Keela's compulsion didn't work before he ever shoved his hand into my chest.

The bedroom door clicks open and I don't bother turning around to see who it is. "I hope you're hungry," Gelby says so casually it's hard to believe he and his brothers were torturing me only hours ago. Or maybe it was days ago. It's hard to know how much time is passing when you're cut off from the world.

He slides a tray of food onto the bed beside me and then looks out the window I'm grateful to have. "Siomha loves to feed us. She was pleased to have a human to cook for. Our food is so different from yours and while we can eat your human fare, it's rare for Siomha to get to prepare an entire human meal in her kitchen."

I take a breath. As much as I'd like to continue ignoring him, I see no real point in it. "Is that what you meant when you said Keela asking Siomha to feed me was going to be a problem?"

He falls silent for a moment, then turns and slides the tray closer to me so he has room to sit on the bed alongside it. "Keela taking an interest in you is the problem." My eyes jump to his and he greets them with a sad smile. "Your attraction to her is obvious, but it isn't novel or even unexpected. You may be wholly innocent, Sean Winkle, and her intervention on your behalf completely justified, but you did not simply fall for a beautiful girl because my sister is not someone a male becomes attracted to. She *is* attraction. Keela..." He hesitates. "She is unlike any others of her kind. All of them have attractive qualities and humans are drawn to them. It's part of their evolution and necessary for the survival of their species. None of them possess the same allure my sister has, though. Keela is different from the rest of her kind because *all* living things are attracted to her. Fae. Ulfr. I've even witnessed Jötnar falling on their knees in front of her, begging for just one kiss."

Jealousy rears its head and I punch it down. Keela may have intervened on my behalf but not until she felt as if I'd been tortured enough. If she cared for me, she would never have let them take me to the dungeon to begin with. "Is that why Haldir behaves the way he does around her? He's in love with his own sister."

Gelby nods slowly. "He is. He can't help it, though, and neither can she. Keela does not control her allure as others of her kind are able to do. When Bishop first brought her here, we didn't know that. *She* did not know. Haldir instantly took to her and it was many years before we realized his possessiveness was due to more than him simply being the brother to her that we were all raised to be."

"Keela is adopted?"

Gelby leans his elbows onto his knees and stares out the window again. "Yes."

I don't know if he's being forthcoming because he feels guilty for what he did to me or if he wants to warn me away from Keela. Either way, his answers regarding her only lead to more questions and remind me of how all of this ties back to her. "What is she? I keep hearing all of these words...Fae, Seelie, Unseelie... What do they all mean? If I'm in this world now, where magic exists and you can put me to sleep with nothing more than a whisper, I want to know what all of you are."

He sighs. "Right. Human. I somehow keep forgetting that."

My spine stiffens. "You mean it wasn't obvious while you were torturing me?"

He straightens, angling his body on the bed to face me. "You're strong, even for a human, but no, we didn't forget what you are. There's more at stake here than what you realize so we had to do what we did. Not to harm you, but to keep our family safe. The Ulfr, the race your friend Collin and his family belong to, are second in loyalty only to my own family. They're protectors and warriors, just as we are. Only, the Ulfr protect themselves and go to war for the highest bidder. Or for the side they think will win. They are of Midgard, your human realm, so they mingle with humans and do sometimes adopt one into their pack. We assume that's what happened with you. The MacKenzie pack took a liking to you and though they did not turn you, they still see you as theirs. Enough that Leah decided to mark you as her mate."

I press the heels of my hands into my eyes. "I am not her mate."

Gelby sighs. "Not yet. But Ulfr have the ability to turn mortals into one of them. It's a painful process and it doesn't always work, so the practice is frowned upon. However, you would be the type of specimen favored by their kind. As I said, you're very strong for a human, even without the magic lending itself to your recovery."

I drop my hands to my lap. "Good to know that my best friend relegated me to being a *specimen*."

Gelby chuckles. "I believe it's Leah you should worry about. Though any male with Alpha blood would be able to change you, it would be her father who approves it. Her marking you means he was, or is, on the verge of doing that. Being Collin's sister, she would know your natural strengths. One could then easily deduce that you'll be a powerful wolf, and there's nothing the Ulfr like more than power."

I shake my head. "Leah and I hate each other. Me becoming a shapeshifting wolf won't make me like her." I swallow. "Will it?"

He shrugs. "The wolf inside of you might decide that it loves the one inside of her. My guess is that Leah put her venom inside you in hopes that when you made the transition, your wolf would be drawn to hers. You'd still be best friends with her brother and with her Alpha blood, you would be an excellent choice as Collin's second when it comes time for him to lead their pack. In essence, with you at her side, Leah's position in the pack would not change, and she also wouldn't have to leave her pack in order to mate well enough to stay in the upper echelon. Even your offspring would have a shot at becoming future pack leaders."

Bile rises in the back of my throat. "I'm a pawn to her. To all of them."

He tugs the tray of food around. It's full of all my favorite things. Extra cheesy lasagna, blueberry pie, corn muffins, and the biggest Ceasar salad I've ever seen. He nudges it toward me. "The Ulfr are not immortal as I am, but they do live much, much longer than humans. It seems Collin is your true friend so if it was he who requested to change you, I would think he only cares to have his best friend with him longer." His eyes darken, a shot of electricity zapping through them. "Leah's treachery is another matter. I intend to lay all her motives bare when she decides to show her face again."

My stomach rumbles so I pick up a corn muffin. "Leah's missing? Keela said you've been talking to her."

He takes one of the corn muffins for himself and smells it before taking a bite. "I've spoken to Leah on the phone but she's attempting to hide from me. Keela can find her, but Rohan is forbidding her from leaving. Rightfully so. My sister is more than capable of taking care of herself under normal circumstances, but these times are anything but normal."

Relief flutters through me to know that Keela is safe, protected, and capable of keeping herself that way. "What exactly is she? If I feel how I do about her and she can't compel me to stop, I need to know what she is."

He glances at the door. "Keela is Vampir. Or what your human stories call a Vampire."

My head swims. I drop the muffin back to the tray. "Blood. She eats blood."

Gelby swipes my muffin. "I don't think blood is as chewy as this muffin, or as good. I believe she only drinks it." A bell chimes and he blinks out of sight. Shouting filters into the room. I race out the door and down the hall, throwing myself against the balcony railing. Rohan and Haldir are flanking Keela, and Gelby is approaching the front door. I turn and race down the stairs, my heart pounding. I reach the bottom of the stairs just as Gelby throws open the two front doors. Standing on the porch is a woman who looks more like a Vampire than Keela does. Her long dark hair falls in straight lines to her waist, almost blending in with the color of her skin. Her eyes are wide and shine like emeralds in the night. Her lips are the color of rum and they're not the only thing about her that's curvy. The sleek black pantsuit she's wearing hugs every mile of curves on her tall frame. She smiles and I shudder. There's no mistake about it, this gorgeous woman is deadly.

"Jofir." Gelby stands aside and waves for her to enter. "Welcome. We were surprised to hear from your father today. Is he well?"

Her shrewd eyes scan the room, first landing on me and then moving across to the others before finding a focal point. Rohan. "He is indeed. When you confirmed for Dokkar that rumors of an attack in Vasilis territory were true, he thought it best to show our support by sending me to assist you." She dips her head to Rohan. "I am at your service."

He steps forward, his hand reaching for the one she's offering. He cups her slender fingers, a sharp intake of breath marking the moment their skin meets. His lips part, a low whisper of words flowing past his lips. "Mia mel..."

The room falls silent, everyone standing so still fear begins to drip through me. I clear my throat, hoping there isn't any kind of magic that can freeze people in place. "Mia mel? That's what you called Keela. What does it mean?"

Nope, they're definitely not frozen. Four sets of eyes are burning through me. Haldir is the only one who doesn't seem upset over my question. He's more relaxed than I've ever seen him and he's...smiling.

Jofir rips her hand away from Rohan and shoulders past him, running her hand down Haldir's arm. "Will you be so kind as to show me to the quarters I was promised? Maybe we can even dine together later. I've heard so much about you, yet I know so little about Dreki." Her eyes flit to Keela. "Other than they have questionable taste. That seems to be a Vasilis family trait. Nothing an unfortunate dragon can be blamed for."

Haldir escorts Jofir back to the door. "Your quarters are next door. I'll take you there, but I'll be dining with Keela later."

The door clicks shut behind them and Rohan makes a noise that shakes the floor beneath my feet. Gelby moves in front of me and throws up one of his electric walls. "He does not know our ways, brother. He meant no harm."

Rohan throws an arm toward me, tendrils of blue smoke rising from all around him. Keela grips his other hand in hers and pulls him toward the fireplace. Rohan blinks out of existence before it ever yawns open for Keela. She treks inside and disappears. Gelby lowers his wall with a forceful exhale. "Odin's wrath is upon us, Sean Winkle, and you just might be the instrument of his destruction."

22

I stare at the fireplace. Gelby wants me to follow him inside but the last time I went in there, I ended up in the dungeon. I glance at the front door. Maybe there's no magical lock on it now. Maybe my two crow friends will help me if I escape. "You can't get out," Gelby answers my question. "Now that you've both entered and escaped, my wards will remain reinforced."

I walk toward the gaping maw of the fireplace. My hands begin to sweat and my breath comes out in shallow spurts. "Can I just wait for you back in my room?"

Gelby waves me forward. "Afraid not. But you have my word that you will not be placed back in the dungeon." His brow furrows. "Unless a new reason for you to be there should arise."

"Great," I mutter, walking past him and shivering against the coolness of the air. "I don't have any choice but to go where you tell me to go, so try not to make up another stupid excuse to lock me up and torture me."

Gelby keeps step beside me. "Our actions may seem unfair to you but you have not seen what we have."

I squint at the walls, trying to see the markings Keela used. There's no point in arguing with Gelby about what's fair. The conviction in his voice tells me he'd torture me all over again if he thought that would get him the answers he's looking for. Must be nice to have that kind of power because nothing I ask ever results in an explanation that explains the whole of my situation to me. "This cave doesn't look like a natural formation. Did your family dig this out?"

Gelby looks around the dimly lit stone hallway. "In a way, I suppose we did. I've never really thought of it as a cave though."

I rub at the gooseflesh puckering my skin. "What do you consider it?"

He reaches out and runs his fingers along the stone surrounding us. "This is a world unto itself. It connects our home in this realm with that of our home in Alfheim."

I look behind me at the length of darkened corridor. "Do you mean...we're not on Earth anymore?"

Gelby chuckles. "At the moment, we're technically not anywhere. I suppose you've never heard of a pocket world?" I shake my head and he sighs. "No, I supposed not, since it's our job to ensure humans don't know about such things. You're a testament to how good my family is at their job, Sean Winkle."

I swallow. "Are you a shapeshifter, too?"

"Hardly," he huffs. "The Ulfr are powerful and some of them have learned to wield magic, but Álfar are born with magic. Some have more than others and if we want to wield what's all around us, we need a wand and a lot of practice. But in a battle, one Álfr is worth ten wolves." His lips turn up. "Maybe only five, but still, they answer to us, not the other way around."

"And what exactly is an Álfr? Or Álfar?"

He grins. "Álfr is singular. Álfar is the name of my people as a whole. Your children's stories call us elves."

I suck in a breath. "I was right! Bishop is Santa Claus."

Gelby's grin fades. "Just as the Álfar bear little resemblance to what you humans depict in your stories, Bishop has little in common with your Santa Claus. We allow the human stories, though, because while there are many different forms of Álfr, my family's duty is to keep magic hidden from your race. Throughout the centuries, we've found that one way to keep adult humans from believing in us is to make ourselves the stuff of children's stories. Once you humans reach puberty, you want to separate yourselves from childhood so much that you deny magic of your own free will." He gives me a sideways glance. "For the rest, Bishop keeps lists of who's been in direct contact with magic, and for those people we pop into their homes and give them a dose of a powerful magical forgetting spell. Once a year, we douse most of Midgard in it. Though our sleigh hardly has room to take every child a toy."

I stop and Gelby chuckles. "I'm kidding. Bishop rides Sleipnir, his horse. Pete is the only one who travels by sleigh and he doesn't like children. Or humans."

He disappears around the end of the corridor. I follow him into the billiards room. "Who is Pete?" My words trail off when my eyes land on Keela. She slams her fist against the wall and it shimmers as it did before, revealing all manner of sharp and pointy weaponry. She rips the two daggers from their spot and stalks off down the corridor on the far side of the billiards room. Rohan yanks a long sword from the wall and stomps off after her.

Gelby rubs his hands together. "Forget Pete. This is going to be good." He grabs my arm and before I can stop him, he portals us.

My stomach flips and I'm thankful I didn't eat the lasagna. Seconds tick by and my backside slams into a chair. Gelby is next to me with his feet kicked up on a knee-high wall in front of the two movie theater chairs we're sitting in. He offers me the tub of popcorn in his hands. "Don't freak out. I promise I won't let them kill each other."

"What?" I snap my attention to the arena in front of us. "What is this place?"

"Our training room," Gelby answers.

I want to ask what they're training for but the side door bursts open and Keela stomps to the middle of the floor, spinning and throwing one of her knives at Rohan who is barely past the threshold. He bats the knife away and in a blur, Keela is behind him, both daggers back in her hands and her booted foot planted at the base of Rohan's spine. He stumbles forward, spinning and slicing his blade through the air at the same time. The tip skims across Keela's abdomen and blood blooms across her stomach. I jump out of my seat, swaying as my noodle weak legs want to give out on me. "Darn you, Gelby."

He yanks the back of my shirt and pulls me down into my chair. "She's fine. Sit, and watch her pay him back for that hit."

I sit on the edge of my seat, leaning forward and watching as Keela and Rohan circle one another, striking and matching each other blow-for-blow. Keela blurs out of sight and appears across the room, both of her daggers already soaring through the air. Rohan bats away the one aimed for his chest but the other drills his right hand and he drops his sword. A smile spreads across my face. She's magnificent. "Is she portaling?"

"No." Gelby's voice holds traces of a smile. "Keela has learned to wield strong magic but she is not able to open doorways. She's just really, really fast."

I turn back to the fight. "Impossibly fast." A sickening thought hits me. "How do portals work? Can Arsenious or one of those creatures we saw at Merrymont just open a portal and grab her?"

Gelby tosses the popcorn bucket and it disappears before hitting the floor. "Not here. No one can open portals into our home, or out of it, except for a few within our family. Which is why I was surprised to hear you say that Aether opened one within the confines of our neighborhood. He shouldn't have been able to do that but I did find evidence of it once I looked."

My throat constricts. Keela killed someone and that someone being a prisoner doesn't make me feel any better about it, since I was a prisoner, and innocent. Still, to think of her in danger... "That means she isn't safe here. Or anywhere."

Gelby snaps his fingers and the knee wall in front of us disappears. "Not even you can break through my magic now, so Keela is safe with us. But look at her, Sean Winkle. Do you think my sister will get forced into a portal as easily as you did? Twice?"

I watch the smile curve Keela's lips and ignore the one spread across Rohan's face. He's recovered his sword but his hand is still dripping blood. Keela spreads her arms out to her sides and the shadows peel away from the walls, every corner of the room brightening as the center of the arena grows dark. Rohan tosses up a ball of magic that shines brightly against the darkness but Keela is no longer where she was. The shadows swirl and Rohan crouches low. Watching. Waiting. Like a black widow, Keela drops from above and slams the hilts of her daggers against the tops of Rohan's shoulders. He drops to one knee and grabs her wrist, slinging her overtop of him and slapping the flat edge of his blade against her throat. She lies on her back, panting, as he looms over her, nearly straddling her middle as his own chest heaves. He slowly lifts the blade from her throat, looking at her the way a man in love would. He gets to his feet and extends his hand to her. "Well done, m...Keela."

She shoves the daggers against her pants and the fabric molds like a sheath around them. "You are just beginning, brother, and you will make all things right."

He draws her into a hug and I shift uncomfortably. "Touching," a female voice chimes from the door at the side of the room. It's Jofir.

Rohan releases Keela and walks toward Jofir. She turns and strolls right back out the door. Haldir gives his brother another big smile. "The MacKenzie pack has delivered the witch to the gray house. Jofir will meet you there, unless you'd like me to keep her entertained while you continue to play with Keela."

I look at Gelby. "There are a lot of things about what Haldir just said that I need answers to, but first, what happened to suddenly make him start smiling? Is the dragon broken?"

Gelby claps me on the back. "Ignorance is bliss, Sean Winkle, and yours sure is making this a heck of a lot more fun for me." He motions for me to follow Keela and I unfortunately don't have to be asked twice. She slips out the door ahead of us, Haldir hot on her heels. Gelby sighs. "Mia mel would translate as *my love*. Rohan calls Keela that by choice, but typically it is reserved for the soul the fates have assigned to us. Vasilis heirs spend so much time in Midgard that it is sometimes difficult to find what you humans would call a soulmate. Rohan would have eventually been expected to return home to Alfheim in order to search for his mate, he just wasn't in a hurry to find her."

I move through the doorway ahead of Gelby. "Because of Keela."

He enters the corridor and falls in step beside me. "Yes. He knew he'd eventually have to choose another Alfr to further our lineage, but he was hoping to have many years, maybe even decades or centuries with Keela before Bishop ordered him home."

"Centuries?" I shake my head. I guess that's the perk of immortality. You can be with the person you love for so much longer than my parents ever dreamed possible. "Rohan is always with Keela but I didn't realize they were a couple."

Gelby places a hand on my arm, stopping me so I'm forced to face him. "Keela will not have Rohan, or Hal, or anyone. I know you think I am not a friend to you but I am trying to help you. Feel how you want to about Keela, but remember that it is not her but her power that draws you in. The same as the others. She will not choose you because none of you will choose her. Not really. And in Rohan and Hal's case, they have the fates to thank for much of that. The most either of them can hope for is time with her. Time that will end when they find their mates." He glances down the corridor. "If Rohan would have suspected that there could be a chance of Dokkar's daughter being his mate, he would not have been here when she arrived. That's how much love he has for Keela. But now that he has met Jofir and the spark has ignited, he will chase her and only her to the ends of all of Yggdrasil's worlds. Had Keela ever agreed to a love affair with him, she would be devastated right now." He looks at me. "Do you understand?"

I nod. "Haldir will mate as well? And Keela? All of you?"

His normally bright eyes dim with sadness. "Haldir and Keela come from such rare lineage that they may never meet a mate. That is part of why Haldir thinks she should be with him. Despite their closeness, Keela fears rejection if Haldir ever meets his Dreki. Plus, she knows his affection is in large part a result of her allure, so it is complicated for them." He clears his throat. "It would be even more complicated between you and her. Intimacy will drive Keela to feed. Haldir is strong enough to fight her off, you are not. If she were to go into a bloodlust, she would rip out your throat and not stop until every drop of your blood belonged to her." He releases my arm. "My sister is a powerful predator. Never forget that."

23

Gelby is right that I don't trust him as a friend. He's given me little reason to believe I'm anything more than a means to an end. But I am happy to trot alongside him. He's finally giving me the answers I need, and better still, I'm finally outside of the big white house. I look up at the sky. It's as bright and sunny as the day I first arrived at Merrymont, yet everything under it has changed for me. I drop my eyes back to the road and look around the yard of the gray house two doors down. It's one of the homes with the flower garden landscaping and walking up its sidewalk makes you feel like you're strolling through a park. "Your family owns all of these houses?"

Gelby eyes the vehicles parked in the driveway. "We own this neighborhood. The houses are all warded to some degree and serve as guesthouses, meeting rooms, or getaways for us whenever we want privacy from the others."

I walk up the broad wooden steps. "The white house is the main house? Where I have to stay?"

"Yes, you will be staying where we can keep a close eye on you." Gelby points to the blue house next door. "Jofir will be staying there until Rohan has groveled enough to convince her to room with him." Gelby's eyes glint with mischief. "If I know anything about Alfar females, Rohan has a long road of very hard work in front of him."

Gelby opens the door of the gray house and ushers me inside. I walk through the foyer and into the living room. Jofir and Rohan are standing by the window on the left. Haldir is seated on the couch, and a wave of apprehension washes over me at the sight of Keela perched leisurely on the arm of a chair next to the couch Haldir is sitting on. *She would rip out your throat.* Gelby's words play at the forefront of my mind. *My sister is a powerful predator. Never forget that.* She looks up at me and I swallow, turning my head away before I get sucked into her alluring stare. The want I have for her is still alive and well, but now that I know what she is and why I'm feeling this way, I'm going to have to fight myself every time I have the urge to take her in my arms to kiss that bloodsucking mouth of hers.

Leah darts around the corner and I stop in my tracks. "You," I growl at her.

She holds up her hands. "I can explain."

Anger swells in my chest. "You better hope so. Do you know what these people have done to me because of you?"

Liam MacKenzie appears behind his daughter, his voice firm and authoritative. "No. Tell us what the Vasilis did to you while refusing to release my charge."

I look between Leah and him. "Your charge?"

Liam steps around his daughter. "Come. There is much to discuss."

I take a step toward him and then stop myself. "I don't want to be a wolf."

His eyes glow a fierce yellow. "You are too naive to know what you want, and too involved with the Vasilis to make a choice that is best for you. Come to me, Sean. We will talk, and all will be as it should."

Rohan crosses the room. "Our terms were clear when we agreed to let you see the boy. You will speak to him, in front of us, but his release depends on the results of the witch. Until that time, he will not leave with you and you will not attempt to convert him."

Liam's eyes scan the others in the room before coming back to rest on Rohan. "Bishop may be the High Álfr of Midgard and therefore has dominion here, but he has no right to keep me from my charge."

All of the Vasilis, even Jofir, make a noise that says they all disagree with Liam. The air around Rohan sizzles and snaps. He places his hands behind his back, a show of how confident he is in his own power. "The MacKenzie pack has never given us problems. Therefore, we choose to remain as allies. Ones with authority over you. Make no mistake, if we find out you had any involvement in Sean Winkle's spelling, you will answer for your every deception."

Liam steps closer to Rohan, putting on his own power display with his shoulders back and his jaw set. "You made your *authority* clear when you scoured my property and interrogated my pack without cause or provocation. You continue to overstep even now. The boy is *mine*. I have watched over him since the day he was born and you will *not* keep him from his pack."

I wobble and Gelby places a hand on my back. I shake my head. "My pack? I'm a shapeshifter?"

Leah walks toward me. "No. Not yet."

I back away from her. "Stop right there. They told me what you did to me. I'm not your freaking mate, Leah, but you carved me up like I am and guess who got tortured for that? Me. While you're still running around free and spending Daddy's money without a care in the world."

She blanches. "They tortured you?"

Liam growls and a flurry of commotion shoots through the room. Gelby shoves me behind him while Haldir faces off with Liam and Keela stares down Leah. Jofir walks to the center of the room. "Where is the witch? Fetch her, Rohan, before the Ulfr make further fools of themselves. I'm getting bored."

She walks through the house and one by one, everyone else follows her. Gelby grins over his shoulder at me. "For a human, you sure do cause a lot of drama, Sean Winkle."

I rub my face. "For an elf, you're awfully tall. And you sure do use my full name a whole lot."

He chuckles. "Habit. To the Álfar, what humans use as a surname is a depiction of their lineage. It tells how pure their blood is and what power they're capable of possessing. Whereas humans have diluted blood and many recessive genes because of it, Álfar rarely mix races and those who do must alter the names of their offspring." He nods to Rohan and Jofir as we enter the dining room. "It is because of the mate bond. It is rare for us to produce offspring without the bond, and the bond only works for those of us with pure Álfr blood."

My eyes immediately find Keela. One day she may have a mate and a trail of broken hearts behind her. Mine already feels like it's breaking and I've barely spoken to her. It's surreal to feel so convincingly in love with someone, yet know that it's all a hoax, emotions forced on me by a power I can't possibly comprehend. I'm only glad Leah doesn't have such appeal. Or else I'd be begging Liam to change me. I shudder at that thought, thankful for the new voice drawing me away from that line of thinking. I don't want to contemplate what it would be like to feel for Leah what I'm feeling for Keela. "Good of you to join us." At the head of the table, a familiar red braid is perched in a high-back chair.

I suck in a breath. "Is everyone at Merrymont some kind of...nonhuman?"

Leah moves slowly toward me. "Very few humans are permitted and I warned Collin about sponsoring you. Now you're here, and without his protection. That's why I did what I did. I marked you to keep you safe."

Gelby snorts and Leah turns fiery eyes on him. "Yes, I will mate him if he joins our pack, and I can see that convincing him to do that will require us undoing all of the lies you've told him about us."

Gelby runs the back of his hand over her cheek. "I've told him no lies, but you, pretty one, have told him little truth. Let us clear it all up before I join with the witch and break his magic."

"The witch has a name." The girl with the braid stands and motions to the chair beside her. "I'm Monique, and Sean will need to sit here. Gelby Vasilis will sit here." She points to the chair on the other side of her, looking at him. "I'll need you to funnel your magic into my crystals and I'll draw it out from there."

He leans forward and presses a kiss to Leah's cheek before taking his seat on the opposite side of Monique, a smirk on his face as he watches the blush creeping up Leah's neck as she avoids eye contact with her father.

I shift my gaze to Keela. She's watching me...the way a predator would. Rohan moves to my side. "Sit. Monique comes from the Völva line. She's one of the few who can channel our magic and use it as her own. We are stronger than her, but she draws and utilizes magic in a different way than we do."

I swallow. "So I'm being tortured again?"

Liam growls and Rohan shakes his head. "This will be different. As I said, the Völva isn't as powerful as we are and even when wielding our magic, she will not be doing so with the same raw intensity we do." He motions to the chair beside Monique. "Sit. The day is growing long and there is still much to do."

I look at Liam and he nods. "The Álfris telling the truth. No harm will come to you while I'm here."

"Same." Keela pushes off the wall and walks to the table where Leah is standing beside her father, her head down. "Some people may continue to underestimate you, but I give you my personal guarantee that you will survive this and go on to have many, many shots, Sean."

Leah's head snaps up and she looks from Keela to me and back at Keela before swinging her head around to Gelby. He grins at me. "Sit down, Sean. The MacKenzie pack has some things to explain to you before we begin."

Monique plops into her chair with a groan and I take my seat beside her, watching Liam fold his hands on top of the table before looking around, waiting for the rest of the people in the room to be seated. Rohan sits beside me and Jofir sits on the opposite side of the table, two chairs away from Liam. Leah sits on her dad's right and Haldir moves to the doorway we walked through to enter the dining room, standing in front of it like a sentinel. Keela paces around the table and comes to a stop behind me. I swallow, suddenly too aware of how delicate the skin of my throat is.

"Days before you were born," Liam begins, "I received a package containing a crystal and various other gems. There was even gold. At first, I had no idea where the box came from or why I had received it. Then my wife recognized the crystal as one that the Álfar and the Fae use to communicate with Alfheim when they are here on Midgard. I consulted with the local witch coven." He nods to Monique. "The Völva are powerful seers and they confirmed what the crystal was but they were not able to trace where it originated from. All I was ever able to do was use the crystal to retrieve the message from inside it. One that told me to seek out the child, Sean Winkle, and guard him with my life." He meets my stare. "I was surprised to find you were a human. I had originally assumed otherwise but after orchestrating your dad's transfer to the car lot in Richlands and ensuring your mom had a job as well, I sent the Völva to inspect you many times."

I gasp. "Inspect me? You got my parents their jobs?"

Liam nods. "If I was to be tasked with watching you, I needed you close by. Having a son of my own who was your age, I knew Collin would eventually be able to help me keep tabs on you."

I bolt out of the chair but Keela presses her hands to my shoulders and pushes me back into the seat. I resist the urge to place my hands over hers. "You forced Collin to be my friend?"

Liam's lip curls. "No. I discouraged my pack from being friendly with you. All we needed to do was keep an eye on you and that could be done without interacting with you. Collin took it upon himself to disobey me."

Leah looks up at me and I meet her eyes. The way she ridiculed Collin for being friends with me makes sense now. She was following Daddy's orders. So was everyone else in Richlands because nearly everyone there is related to Liam MacKenzie in some way. I was surrounded by shifters and had no idea. Collin never let them keep us from being friends, though. I guess I should feel good about that.

Leah's eyes move to where Keela's hands still rest on my shoulders. Keela's fingers flex and Leah looks away, muttering, "Unlike here, there were no threats to you in Richlands, Sean."

"Which is why we grew complacent," Liam admits. "Each year, on the eve of the anniversary of having received that first box, I would get another, full of riches that served as payment for my pack overseeing your continued safety. For the first dozen years of your life, I attempted to trace the origin of the sender. The magical wards on the box prevented the coven from tracking it. Each crystal merely contained photos of you. I took that to mean that whoever wanted you guarded was also watching over you, but no matter how much we looked for magical signatures or foreign scents in our territory, we always walked away empty-handed. The witches found nothing magical or special about you, so eventually, I accepted that someone was willing to pay handsomely for your safety and that since you were living in my territory, it was an easy and very lucrative job for my family."

"Glad I helped you buy another yacht while my parents worked themselves to death in order to buy me the designer clothes your *family* made fun of me for not having," I snap.

He shrugs. "I won't apologize for taking payment for a job I was hired to do. Your father wouldn't take money from me and you wouldn't take it from Collin. We've always tried to make sure your needs were met." He glances at his daughter. "Our nature is different than yours, but like Collin, all of the MacKenzie pack learned not only to respect you, but to accept you." He meets my eyes again. "I never made demands of you, Sean. I let you do whatever you wanted and felt no need to reveal the pack to you because there didn't seem to be any reason to. There is nothing we could have done to save your parents. Your father's death was too quick and your mother too weak to survive a transformation. If I could have saved her for you, I would have. Ulfr are not immortal as these others are." He waves a hand around the room. "But we age much more slowly than humans."

Betrayal bleeds through me and my fists clench. "You want to make me one of you so you can keep getting a big fat paycheck each year."

Liam's big hand folds overtop of his daughter's. "No. Collin and Leah have both asked for you to join us and I've agreed to allow it, but only if you choose it. Collin planned to tell you about us this year but he's been called away on pack business, and unfortunately my daughter's eagerness put the cart before your horse, and now here you are. But she is not entirely to blame. As I said, we had the witches inspect you and they found no magic or spell attached to you. Leah has kept a close eye on you since Collin has been gone and she's detected nothing new in your scent. We're at a loss when it comes to giving these Vasilises the answers they are so impatiently demanding. We have no idea how or when you were spelled, the same as we have no idea who tasked us with your care."

Monique leans forward. "My family didn't have the power of the Vasilis to channel when they checked you before. So let's begin. Collin's friendship with you might have made his family's job too easy, but it's making my life miserable. I expect you to move out of my dorm, Sean Winkle. Your absence is all the payment I need for this."

She begins to chant and ropes of sizzling blue magic flow from Gelby's fingertips into a trio of crystals set up in front of him and Monique. I hold my breath. They can deny it all they want, but I can already tell this is going to hurt.

Keela

Sean's muscles tense and as much as I want to reassure him, I have to remove my hands from his shoulders so I don't interfere with the witch's magic. I should never have touched him to begin with. Leah's scent has finally faded but the memory of it still clings to my nostrils. She slept with Gelby and still has the nerve to sit across from Sean and give him her puppy dog eyes while my brother sits feet away. If Gelby didn't look at Leah the way he does, I wouldn't care that her attention is on someone else. But Gelby normally doesn't fall for anyone, not even me, and the person Leah wants to get with next happens to be someone I've fallen for.

I drink in Sean's scent, opening my senses so I can pick up on his many emotions. Gelby shouldn't have brought him to the arena. Fear has hung like a cloak around Sean's shoulders since we left there. A fear deeper than what I smelled on him in Alberich's lair. I ache for him now as I did then. Unlike the rest of my kind, my heart still beats, and today it thumps in tune with Sean's.

Gelby's magic fills the three crystals and the witch begins to siphon it out, her chants growing louder. Stronger. I flex my fingers. She's supposed to be able to see the source of Sean's magic, unweave whatever spell is on him, and look into his future. If what she sees there is him mating the Ulfr, my brothers better hope they can stop me before I reach Leah MacKenzie. My bloodlust is growing. I fed from Alberich this morning because I can't take anything more from Gelby. I can't feed from *anyone* my body will mold to. Alberich's stench and his mouthful of teeth are as unappealing as he is unappetizing. The complete opposite of Sean Winkle. If it is his magic drawing me to him, then it's best for all of us if it's broken. If I'm still drawn to him after the spell is removed, Gelby will have to stand guard as I feed from Sean's veins. I don't want to kill him, I want to lose myself in him time and again.

Sean groans and Gelby flicks his eyes to mine. I've told no one of my feelings for the human but my brothers know me too well. Rohan is occupied with Jofir, but Haldir is still occupied with me and I'll receive another lecture from him once this is over. Maybe two, if I end up killing the wolf who is watching Sean with a pained expression. A sound escapes my chest. Leah looks up. I hold her stare. She wants to look away but she's too stubborn to give up easily. Especially in front of her father. I bare my teeth at her and she whimpers. Haldir crosses the room and rests a hand against my lower back. I let it stay there because to remove it would mean moving away from Sean. He leans forward and holds his head.

I look at the witch. "What's happening?"

She shakes her head, her eyes growing wide as tendrils of red smoke lift away from Sean's arms. Every hair on his body is standing on end and I can feel the panic rising in him, and in the witch. She screams and a blinding flash of light explodes out of Sean. His chair tips backward. I catch him but the witch has no such luck. The blast launches her into the wall, the drywall cracking and falling on her in chunks. Gelby's magic holds him in midair and everyone else is shoved back from the table.

Gelby lowers to the ground and checks on the witch. Leah yelps and points at Sean. "He's on fire!"

I spin his chair. There's a flame licking at the side of his face, just in front of his ear. I snuff it out. "Are you okay?"

He blinks his glassy eyes. "What in the hell was that?"

I look at the witch. She stands on shaky legs, reeking of fear. "Exactly. What in the hell are you?"

Sean looks around the room, still in shock. "Me? I did this?"

Rohan checks on Jofir. "Monique, contact your coven. Let them know we're on our way. Whatever it takes, I want his magic broken. Today."

I lift Sean from his chair. "Can you walk?"

He glances at Haldir. "You are *not* carrying me." I begin to offer to carry him but Sean's eyes swing back to mine, the haze of shock wearing off. He pulls his hands free of mine. "I'm good. I can walk."

I move away from him and leave the house. Haldir follows me. I walk to the end of the driveway. "Don't."

He runs his big hands over my shoulders and down my arms. "You force me away but even now, I can feel the fates orchestrating our destiny. Rohan has his mate, the human will have a short life, and you and I will be together. This was meant to be, Keela. I love you, and you love me."

I close off my senses and slow my heart rate. "I do love you, but not in the way my allure forces you to love me. You must search for your true mate, Haldir. It is the only way to survive me."

I remove myself from him and wait for the others in the garage. Rohan portals inside with Jofir, opening the passenger door of a sleek black SUV. She takes one look at me and rips the door from his grip, getting inside the vehicle and slamming the door shut behind her. Rohan sighs. "I don't suppose you would mind riding with Gelby instead of me?"

I scan the door to the seat that's been mine for so long, I can't remember a time when I wasn't Rohan's shotgun rider. How quickly things change. Each day, Rohan will find me less appealing. Each day, he will withdraw from me until Jofir is happy and I am alone. "The human will ride with Gelby and me. Haldir goes with you."

Rohan rubs his tired face. "We need to talk, Keela. Let's just get through today and then we'll take some time to ourselves. Hopefully Bishop will be back by then. He will need to speak with Dokkar about Jofir and what her place with us will be now." Sorrow coats his eyes and I look away. We knew he would one day find his true mate, and I always knew that I loved him and Haldir too much to ever give them the physical relationship they wanted to have with me. Even so, it hurts to lose him. Had I been his lover, Jofir may be in as much trouble of losing her life as Leah MacKenzie is.

Gelby walks into the garage with Leah and Sean trailing behind him. Leah's lips are moving a mile a minute as Sean listens to her intently.

Haldir is behind them, his eyes on me. "Hal," Rohan calls out. "You're with me. The rest are with you, Gelby."

Gelby nods. "I sent Liam and the witch on ahead, but Leah wanted to stay with Sean."

Haldir brushes against me as he passes by to go to Rohan. Gelby watches us both, shaking his head and pointing to the second SUV. "Load up, people. Whoever spelled my boy Sean is really starting to piss me off. I'm not just going to break their magic, I'm going to take it." He gets into the driver's seat and slams his door. I've always wondered if the strength of Gelby's magic is what makes him immune to me. If Sean's is stronger, why is the human still attracted to me?

Sean holds the back passenger door open for Leah. She gets inside and Sean glances at me before jogging around and getting in the backseat behind Gelby. Beside *Leah*. I may not be as docile as the wolf, and Sean is right to fear me, but I will not let the wolf have him in my presence. Sean Winkle is *mine*.

I barely contain my rage as I march to the SUV and tear open the back passenger door. "Move." Leah slides across the seat toward Sean. I hear the door's metal crunching under my grip. "Front. Now."

Gelby reaches back and tugs Leah over the console. "Quick tip. When I'm pissed, I get even. When my sister is pissed, you get dead. So get the hell out of her way and stay out of it."

I climb into the vehicle and shut my door. Leah buckles into the front seat and Sean puts his hand on his door. "Stay," I order, hearing the thickness of his spit as he swallows down his nervousness.

Gelby starts the engine. "Alrighty then, let's get this road trip started. I have a feeling it's going to be a real blast."

Sean

If the clock on the dashboard is right, we've been driving for an hour and fifteen minutes. In total silence. No one has said a single word. It's because of Keela. I look at her profile for the sixtieth time. She's definitely angry but I have no idea who that anger is directed at. Leah, for sure, but maybe Gelby and me too. I look down at her hand resting on the seat beside her. I'd love to reach over and fit my fingers between hers. More than that, I'd like to pull her to me and fit my arms around her. I meet Gelby's eyes in the rearview. He shakes his head and I turn to face out the side window before I do something really stupid with a Vampir who looks like she's hankering to rip out someone's throat. "Leah, when is the last time you spoke to Collin?"

She doesn't answer. I look at her. She tosses me a glare over her shoulder. "Don't do that," I scold. "You and your family put me through enough and I haven't been able to get a hold of Collin since he left."

She blows out a hard breath. "You heard Dad. Collin is away on pack business."

Gelby leans toward her. "You might as well answer the question because Rohan already ordered that Collin MacKenzie be hunted down."

She glares at him. "Leave my brother alone. He's doing nothing wrong."

I sit forward. "Then tell us where he is."

She chews on her bottom lip. "We were hired for a job that Dad wanted Collin to do."

"What job?" Gelby asks.

She looks at me, her eyes sliding over to Keela before straightening back to Gelby. "I can't give you details because I don't know all of them. All I know is it's a lost and found kind of thing. Next to Dad, Collin is our best tracker, and Dad thought the job would take too long for him to do himself so he ordered Collin to take it." She gives me a small shrug. "I tried to do it since Collin wanted to be here with you, but Dad said the job was too important and that Collin can finish his studies later. I guess if he misses too much school and flunks this year, that'll give you and him two years together at Merrymont instead of only one."

I sit back with a huff. "I'm pretty sure I won't be passing a single class at Merrymont, let alone a full year."

The vehicle falls quiet again and I let it stay that way. Every hope and dream I ever had is gone now. There's no coming back from all of this. Gelby follows Rohan's SUV up a gravel driveway that's shaded by towering magnolia trees. I wonder why Gelby and Rohan didn't just portal us here but I assume the reason is the same as why no one else is allowed to portal onto Vasilis land. The vehicles curve around the circular driveway and Gelby parks behind Rohan. Everyone begins exiting the vehicles. Keela's hand darts to mine. "Wait."

I freeze. So do Gelby and Leah. Keela growls at them. "Leave us."

Gelby meets my eyes. I shake my head and he looks at his sister. "Don't make me have to zap you."

Leah's fearful eyes meet mine before she closes her door and Gelby does the same. I sit perfectly still, with Keela's hand covering mine. She slides her touch away and my muscles tighten even more. Having her hand on mine was oddly calming. I glance at her. She's facing forward and her profile no longer looks angry. It looks sad. Guilt races through me. I've been so focused on what's happening to me that I haven't taken enough time to consider how she's feeling.

I settle back against my seat and decide I should talk first. I don't love bringing up her ex, especially since he's an ex by death, but I've been wanting time alone with her and I finally have it. Mostly. I'm aware of the others not too far away beyond the dark tint of our windows. "I've lost people I care about so I know there's nothing I can say to make you losing Aether any easier to deal with, but I am sorry you're having to go through losing someone close to you. Losing my parents was hard enough. I can't imagine having to live through the loss of a girlfriend."

"Aether was a good friend to me," she answers softly. "But I was not in a relationship with him." She faces me. "I did not love him in that way, and I too am sorry for the loss you've suffered in your life. Many things have happened to you that you do not deserve."

I smile at her. "I think the same is true for you."

She slides across the seat. "You know what I am, and now you are afraid of me?"

Heat surges through me at her nearness. My heart hammers and I can't stop myself from licking my lips. "I...um..."

She slides onto my lap, her fingers tracing along the column of my neck. "I want you, too."

I don't move as she leans in, her nose running along my skin where her fingers just blazed a trail over my heated neck. Need and want tug at me and my hands slide over her, my fingers digging into her hips as I pull her closer, my body responding to every move she makes. I reach up and fist her hair in my hand, doing what I've wanted since the moment I saw her. I drag her mouth to mine. She kisses me back, her legs moving to straddle me as I beg for more of her, kissing her to own her, not only to taste her.

I groan against her mouth. She's better than anything I've fantasized about, my whole body is ready to explode. She pulls her lips from mine, dropping her mouth to my neck. I tilt my head to rest on the back of the seat, my chest heaving as her lips work over my skin. I dig my fingers into her backside and hold her down on me. I don't care if she can rip me apart with her teeth. I want her. "We need to go someplace private."

"Break your magic." Her voice is husky against my ear.

I lower my mouth to her shoulder and taste her skin, returning her favor by kissing my way up the column of her neck. "What?"

She cups my face, her lips grazing mine, breath heavy and panting. "Help them break your magic. If you do, I will come to you."

I capture her mouth, the swell of her breasts against my chest driving me mad. "I don't know anything about magic, Keela. All I know is this." I cover her mouth with mine again, deepening the kiss. I'm so turned on that if she needs to feed, I'll slice open my own veins for her. She can lap up my blood while I get her naked because there's not a damn thing this woman can do that will douse the flame I have for her. If there's one thing I know is true, it's that.

Keela moves and she's across the seat and standing outside the SUV before I have a chance to stop kissing the air in front of me. I lower the hands I was just holding her in less than a second ago and raise a brow at her. She looks down. "Break the magic and I will come to your bed every night. That's the only way."

I lick at the taste of her that's still on my lips. "Why?"

The question is out of my mouth but Keela is gone. Gelby fills the spot she was just in. "You okay?"

I look down at my too tight jeans. "No. I'm going to need minute."

He moans. "Yeah, I think my sister does too, but there's a dragon out here wishing for your death so use Haldir's face as a cold shower and get inside the lodge already."

elby wasn't exaggerating about Haldir. I'm not sure if the Dreki can breathe fire but if he can, I'm about to be nothing more than a pile of ashes. I close my door and make my way to where Gelby is waiting at the front of the long lodge that looks like a typical ranch-style home, but only it stretches at least a hundred yards. I rub the back of my neck, mostly to tamp down the heat of Haldir's stare. "This is the witch coven?"

Gelby nods knowingly and opens the door. "He'll wait here for Keela to return."

"Return?" I look around. "Where did she go?"

Gelby shrugs. "I keep a tracking spell on her but I think she could use some privacy right now." He glances at me as we walk through the long hallway we entered into. "Just so you know, all of us have really good hearing. Especially the Dreki. He smells a lot of things too. Like lust."

It's my turn to shrug. "Keela started that and I'm never going to deny her. I couldn't care less what your brother thinks. If she wanted him, she'd have him."

Gelby points at a set of double doors on my right. "It isn't that simple. I told you their relationship is complicated."

I enter through the double doors and face him. "Their relationship *is* simple. He's supposed to be her brother. I'm not. If she wants me, I'm hers. But I think she's afraid this magic, or whatever is in me, will hurt her."

Gelby chuckles. "No, Sean Winkle, she is afraid she will hurt you."

I shake my head. "If she was going to hurt me, she would have by now."

He frowns. "There are many different forms of hurt. Keela wants to break your magic so she can compel you to forget her."

The high of finally kissing her fades as his words sink in. "You can't let her do that."

He walks past me. "It is not my choice, nor is it yours."

"We'll see about that," I mutter, following him to the center of the room where a large circle of candles is casting a glow over the hardwood floor. There are a dozen redheads who all look similar to Monique sitting around it. The door opens and I turn to see if it's Keela but it's... "Bonnie?"

The little girl smiles as she walks toward me. "Hello, Sean. Good to see you again."

I blink and rub my eyes. "Bonnie Potter?"

The air around her shimmers and the girl fades away, leaving in her place an older woman with silver hair. "My name is Beatrice, actually, but I thought it would be nice to meet you wearing a familiar face."

Gelby steadies me as I stare at her. Beatrice winks. "No, I didn't really kiss frogs. I just didn't want you trying to kiss me again, because you never kissed me to begin with. I used that illusion in order to gather some genetic material from you."

"Genetic material?"

She folds her hands in front of her. "A biopsy, of a sort."

Monique steps up beside Beatrice. "This is my great grandmother, and I didn't know you were the one the Ulfr hired her to scan until today."

Liam joins us. "You can see that we did try, Sean. Beatrice lived near you in disguise and like us, she could never sense anything nonhuman about you. Nothing was ever out of place around you until you met them." His eyes flick to the Vasilis.

"All the more reason to get this ritual started," Rohan announces. "My family will stay but the Ulfr can go."

Liam snorts. "We'll stay."

Beatrice waves her hands. "No need for hostilities. Everyone is welcome." She steps over the candles and into the circle, motioning for me to join her. "This will not hurt."

I step into the circle. "That's what everyone keeps telling me."

She takes my hands in hers. "This time, I will be your conduit. I will feel what you feel, see what you see, hear what you hear...past, present, and even future." She smiles warmly. "Monique informed us of what happened, but the magic shrouding you will not be stronger than that of my coven. Especially when we're bolstered by that of the Vasilis."

I take a deep breath. "Okay. Tell me what I need to do. I'm ready for this to be over."

The door opens and Keela walks in, followed by Haldir. I try to pull away from Beatrice but she holds onto me. "There will be plenty of time for that later," she whispers. "I need you relaxed and focused on the sound of my voice."

Keela won't meet my eyes so I put my attention back on Beatrice, taking deep breaths and doing my best to cooperate. I need this magic to be broken so that I can have Keela. I'll figure out how to convince her not to compel me later.

"That's good," Beatrice encourages as the other witches each lift a candle and begin to circle us, chanting. She joins in their chant, her voice soft at first, growing stronger as Gelby and Rohan both shoot magic at our circle, forming a vining dome of electricity around the witches and me. Whisps of blue begin to feed from the dome down into the candle that each witch holds. As they walk, sparks skip along the floor and jump onto my legs. Onto Beatrice's long skirt. *Don't be afraid,* I hear her voice in my head. My eyes widen and she smiles at me, her lips still moving in the chant that is growing louder as the witches draw more power from Gelby and Rohan. Beatrice's hair begins to lift from her shoulders and I feel the air spinning around us. The witches on the outside of the circle blur and thunder cracks along the ceiling. Beatrice's hands clamp down on mine, terror blasting through her features as the floor rolls beneath our feet. Screams echo and Beatrice begins to glow. Her head snaps back at an unnatural angle and her mouth opens, light pouring out of her.

"Sean!" Keela yells. I turn to look for her. All around me is a vortex of murky gray air.

"Keela!" I shout, my voice booming as if a cannon just went off.

"Let go of her!" Keela shouts again and I turn back to Beatrice. Her hands are still clamped in mine and her body is lifting off the floor, thick red lines crackling over her skin. I yank my hands free and her body slumps to the floor. I look down at my palms. They're sizzling with red vines of magic, just like the blue ones Gelby and Rohan wield.

"Keela!" I shout, terrified.

"I'm here," she answers, pounding coming from my left. I walk toward the swirling mass of gray, my hand shaking as I reach out to touch it. Sparks jump from my hand. Through the haze, I see Keela. Her eyes widen in shock. "Sean..."

Overwhelming need rips through me. So does anger, lust, hurt...everything, all at once. My body burns from the inside, like it did when Aether shoved his hand into my chest. Aether, the Fae Keela kissed. Touched. Just as Haldir wants to touch her. I throw my head back and shout.

Screaming beats against my ears. My chest heaves, the pain of Keela's betrayal consuming me. She wants to use me and then compel me to forget her. I won't let her. "Mine," I growl, stomping into the swirling mass of gray. Wind whips at my clothes but my vision is clear. Keela is on the other side of this wall, gaping at me. I stalk toward her. "You. Are. Mine."

"Keela!" Haldir sweeps across my vision and takes Keela with him.

I break through the barrier and run after them, more shouting reaching my ears. I smell smoke. See the flames. Feel my body burning. Still, I run. From the room and down the hall. Blue magic slams into me and I fly out the door, finding myself flat on my back outside the lodge. Rohan and Gelby tower over me, each of them shooting thick cords of magic into me. Keela screams and her body dives over mine. Her brothers yell but she wraps herself around me. "Leave him alone!"

"Move away from him," Rohan orders.

"No," she shouts. "He did not attack on purpose."

My head swims and this time I can't hold back the vomit. I shove Keela away and barely get to all fours before hot liquid races up my throat and spews out my mouth.

"The Vampir is right," Beatrice coughs. I look up to find her cradled in Jofir's arms, pale and covered in blood, her skin split open as if she's been roasted on a spit. She waves a shaking hand and Jofir sits her on the ground next to me. Beatrice places a hand on my shoulder. "My dear boy, I had no idea you weren't human."

Another wave of hot bile spews out of me, thick and black. "What is he?" Rohan asks.

Beatrice's hand falls away from me, as if it has no energy to rest there. "Someone went to great lengths to cloak him." I look over and catch a tear trickling down her bloody, soot-covered face. "Had I known you were Fae, I would never have mixed your magic with theirs."

"Fae?" Everyone gasps while I puke up another round of thick black tar.

Beatrice lies back in the grass and looks up at the sky. "A very old and powerful one."

"How can that be?" Rohan mutters. "Fae do not possess Dreki fire."

Dreki fire? I look behind me. The entire lodge, from end to end, is on fire. Flames lick over the roof and out of the windows. Witches are scattered on the lawn all around me. Some stunned. Others crying. Many bloody and bleeding. Keela crouches beside me. Tears well in my eyes. "I did this?"

She nods. "You didn't mean to."

Jofir snorts and Leah races toward us. "Vampir!"

Keela jumps to her feet. "Now is not the time, Ulfr."

Leah rips off her shirt midstride. "Not you! *Them!*" She points behind, her hand becoming a furry leg. Faster than I can blink, the girl is gone and in her place is a snarling wolf. Behind her, an enormous black wolf is tearing through a horde of...Vampires. A boom crackles through the air and a dragon lifts into the sky. Another boom and a net descends overtop Haldir, the heavy metal pinning him to the ground. The more he struggles, the deeper the edges dig into the earth. Gelby and Rohan race forward, their blue magic scattering across the battlefield as Jofir and a handful of witches join the fight. A roar draws my attention to the left where Leah is facing off with another Vampir horde. They're fast. And there are hundreds of them.

"Arsenious," Keela growls from beside me.

I try to sit up. "Where?"

She points toward the wood line beyond where the black wolf, Liam, is doing his best to kill and not be killed. "Stay here."

"No." I reach for her hand but she's gone, racing right into the middle of battle. Her twin blades are in her hands and she moves so fast I lose sight of her, but I know where she's heading. I crawl away from my puke and head for Haldir.

Keela

I should have expected an ambush. Arsenious doesn't give up easily and he knows he can't touch me on Vasilis ground. He knows he can't take me without an army, so he brought one with him. The Vampir king must have been paid nicely to send so many. I call my shadows to me and scream as we race into the battle, cutting and slicing, my shadows obeying my every whim as we mow down our enemies. We are not enough to level the playing field but I only need one kill to count. Arsenious.

I leap over a brother Vampir and stab a blade through his back and into his heart. Kicking him off my blade and racing forward. A portal opens behind Arsenious and he smiles. I fling both my blades. They hurl through the air, entering the portal behind him. It doesn't close. I run for it as hard as I can. A roar breaks through the chaos and I look up. Haldir is free. On his back, a remarkably unburned Sean Winkle yells my name. When the flames burst from his body I thought the witch had killed him. It was Sean who was killing them.

"They will die," a silky voice says from beside me. I turn and face the king himself. I've never met him but Bishop made sure I knew the Vampir who should be my lord. The king holds out his hand. "Come with me, Keela, and the battle is over. Stay, and you will watch them all die, and then I will still take you."

I glance up at Haldir. There is no time to think. I may die this day, but my family will live. I place my hand into the king's. "Take me to Arsenious."

Also By

Beller Ties – A four-book stand-alone romantic suspense collection.

Something So Beautiful

Now And Always

Dawn Of Devotion

Marked By Forever

Hinton Thriller Series – A serial-killer thriller trilogy.

Descend

Smother

Rise

Sierra: A Modern Psychological Thriller

Eyes Of Midgard series ***Book 2*** coming **March 1, 2024**. Join the mailing list for early release news!

Acknowledgements

"The unknown is where you will grow into the person you know you can truly be." ATGW

Thank you for reading my first foray into a fantasy world. When I started writing, I thought I knew where the story was heading. I was wrong. The characters revealed themselves and told their own story. I did my best to accurately record what they showed me, something I would have no shot at without the kindness, professionalism, and direction of my editor. Thank you, Anita! Without Proof Positive, I'd be lost in a sea of mismatched words.

Special thanks to my husband. One day, I'll stop shutting myself away, ignoring the world while my muse runs amok. One day... Maybe. Probably. Okay, it's highly unlikely but you're not going to read this anyway, so it doesn't need to be a blood oath.

To my son, daughter-in-law, sister-in-law, grandpups, grand-demon-kitty, and sweet Sadie Jo, all of you fill my cup. You, my dear reader, make that cup overflow. Thank you! I can't wait to see what comes next in this trilogy and I hope that you can't either.

About the Author

Lee Dawna is a thriller and suspense author, and host of the Immortal Monsters Podcast. An avid traveler and outdoorswoman, you may bump into her along a remote trail where a meandering stream whispers her next story.

Visit **LeeDawnaBooks.com** for more on what the author is up to lately, and to **join her mailing list** for special announcements.

Find her on YouTube @ImmortalMonsters and @LeeDawnaBooks, and on Patreon @ Patreon.com/leedawna